THE BOUNTY HUNTERS

WRONG BULLET WRONG MAN

Paul L. Thompson

PAUL L. THOMPSON

Copyright ©2023 by Paul L. Thompson

ISBN: 9798852035493

All rights reserved. This book may not be duplicated in any way without the express written consent of the publisher, except in the form of brief excerpts or quotations for the purposes of review. The information contained herein is for the personal use of the reader and may not be incorporated in any commercial programs or other books, databases, or any kind of software without written consent of the publisher or author. Making copies of this book or any portion of it, for any purpose is a violation of United States copyright laws. This is a work of fiction. Names, characters, places, and incidents either are the product of the author's imagination or are used fictitiously. Any resemblance to actual persons, living or dead, events, or locales is entirely coincidental.

FOREWORD

Casey Pascoe had followed two men all the way from New Mexico toward Russellville Arkansas. When those two men cut north at Goodnight Texas, Casey couldn't figure why they wasn't still headed for Arkansas. Weeks later in Cheyenne Wyoming, Sheriff Coleman was surprised to learn Casey was a bounty hunter from New Mexico, sent after these men by Sheriff Daskalas of Albuquerque.

"Why in the world would any sheriff send a kid after two robber killers."

Casey looked at him. "Cause he knew I'd get um. If you'll hold um overnight, I'll get what's left of this money over to Wells Fargo an' pick them two up in the morning. Right now, I've gotta send ah telegram to Albuquerque. Been gone over ah whole month."

"Why's that?'

"So Gus an' my folks'll know I got um at last an's still alive an' headed home. Got two in Santa Rosa Gus'll have to send for."

"They'll be here and fed. Taking um back by horse er train?"

"Train, I've been in the saddle for well over ah month. I have to wire home and let my brother know I got um. One of um shot him right off. He's okay."

CHAPTER ONE

Travis and Casey Pascoe were in Albuquerque, picking a few things up for their mother. When that was done, Casey said, "Let's stop by the Liberty Saloon for one cold beer before headin' back."

"Dad gum Casey, now you read minds!"

They walked in saying howdy to Chris and Milly, just as Sheriff Gus walked in behind them. Gus smiled, "I see you boys got thirsty the same time as I did. Do I buy, or do y'all?"

"You do Gus, we bought last time."

"One thing about it, you both have good memories. Milly, three beers."

Just as they sat to drink, a young boy came running in. "Sheriff Daskalas, a telegram just came in for you. I was told to hurry and find you, it's important."

Gus handed the boy a dime and took the telegram. Casey saw the look on his face and asked, "Trouble?"

"Sure enough could be. Four men just robbed the bank in Bernalillo, shot the teller and got away with just over twenty thousand dollars. Says they headed this way for sure."

Travis said, "Heck, I'd say we could meet um somewhere close to Alameda, if we hurry."

Gus said, "I'll have to get my horse. I guess by you saying we, you and Casey are coming along."

"Heck yeah, there might be a reward, and I was wondering where I was going to get enough money for an all-day sucker. Let's go."

Twenty minutes later they took the stage road headed north. Casey asked, "Think they might stop in Alameda an' maybe eat? Er hit the saloon?"

Gus smiled, "Your guess is as good as mine. All we'll know is its four men, with no descriptions and I'd say they'll be on give out horses. We just have to make sure it's them and not four cowboys riding in just to have some fun."

Travis said, "Ain't never shot the wrong man yet."

Not quite an hour later they were walking their horses slowly up the street in Alameda, looking at every horse, rider or at a hitch rail.

Gus said, "Doesn't look as if they've made it yet."

Casey looked on north as far as he could see up the road. "Yeah, er they just made it look like they was headed for Albuquerque, but turned back east when they got out of sight an' headed torge Placitas."

"Could'a done that I reckon 'cause they had plenty ah time to beat us here an' we shor didn't meet um."

Travis asked, "Then what'll we do now?"

"Go back to that café and have a cup of coffee watching the street. They don't show up, we'll head back for Albuquerque."

Two hours later they were back in Albuquerque. Casey and Travis said they had to get on home by dark. Due east of Alameda, the Lee twins, Louis and Lindal sat in a sandy arroyo drinking whiskey and laughing with the Morgan brothers.

Louis said, "Told y'all with the sheriff's help it would be no trouble robbin' that bank. I'd say we now have us five er eight thousand dollars apiece."

Reese said, "Yeah, but you havin' to shoot that stupid teller, he dies it could get bounty hunters er even U.S. Marshals on our trail. Yeah, an' splitin' half the money with Gomez wadn't right. He should'a only got a share, even split."

"It was his idea, so, we just don't leave um a trail. Now wadn't I right about ridin' down that road torge Albuquerque then one at ah time headin' upon this east mesa. We ain't see no posse er nobody else that even looks like they's after us. We'll hug these foot hills and'll stay six er so miles east of Albuquerque. We'll head up Tijeras Canyon an' ride due east to Santa Rosa. Nobody'll think of lookin' east, nobody."

Charlie said, "Yeah, but we could'a gone up to Placitas an' up the east side ah these mountains. Nobody would'a seen us goin' that'a way."

Lindal said, "There you go Charlie, not thinkin'. Most everybody in Placitas knows ever one of us includin' our horses. We've got drunk up there plenty ah times."

"Oh, yer right. What's yore grandma gonna think when y'all don't ever show back up?"

Louis laughed, "Be damn glad to be rid of us I'd say!" He laughed and took a long drink off that bottle.

"Reece, open us ah couple cans of them beans an' break me off a chunk of that bread."

****

Casey and Travis got home in time to help Joel with the chores and Tiny walked from the chicken coop with a basket of eggs. "Did you go off and forget to get my…"

"No Mama." Casey reached behind and handed her a heavy sack.

"My goodness, I don't tell you to bring the whole store!"

"No Mama, we just didn't want to be sent back to town tomorrow."

They had dismounted as Tiny asked, "Are you getting smart with me? Well, are you?"

"No Mama, if you'll look in the sack, I think you'll like it."

She peeked in, "Ahhh, that's so sweet of you. Now get those horses unsaddled and help your dad. Supper will be ready by the time you're thru with chores and get washed up."

The next morning before eight o'clock, Gus's deputy came riding up to the Pascoe's. Joel had just walked from the barn. "Step down, Randy."

"Thanks, got some papers here for Travis and Casey. Gus thought maybe they'd be interested."

Joel looked at them. "Ugly suckers if I do have to say so." He turned and whistled.

Travis and Casey stepped from the barn and Joel handed Travis all those papers. "Be darn! Not only do we got names of them four robbers, we have pictures of um and descriptions of all four horses. That red and white paint can be spotted from ah long way off. It was the

Lee's grandma Hodges came up with the pictures and even said they might be headed for their grandpa Lee's in Arkansas. Casey, think we could catch um before they get that far?"

"Might if we don't stand here jawin'."

Joel said, "Y'all get saddled. I'll have your mother get yore travelin' gear together."

****

The Lees and Morgans had slept way too late as they had finished off that bottle of whiskey last night. They had just now topped out Sedillo Hill and started down the east side.

Lindal asked, "We gonna stay on this stage road an' swing thru Estancia, er not?"

"Not! Too far out'a the way when Santa Rosa if due east a hundred miles er so. It'll take two weeks er better gettin' to grandpas now. Two maybe three days to Santa Rosa and another three to Amarillo. We'll rest the horses a few days when we get there."

Charlie laughed, "Yeah, my butt's already tired."

Twenty minutes later, Randy, Travis and Casey headed north toward the stage road. Randy said, "I'll let Gus know y'all went after um. They see y'all coming they just might start shooting."

"Why? Heck, they won't know but what we're ah couple ah cowboys. I just wish we had some idea of which they went when they left Bernalillo. But if they's headed east, maybe they'll stop in Santa Rosa an' we can catch up."

Travis said, "I'll say they'll stop there. Onliest town in over ah hundred miles. With all that bank money they'll want'a stop an' have ah few drinks."

They topped a long sloping hill and started down the north said, still several hundred yards from reaching that stage road.

They were in a slow lope and saw as four horses loped past headed east. Casey stood in his stirrups. "Tell me by dog that's them! One's on a red an' white paint."

They kicked those horses into a run and in no time turned east on that stage road. They were gaining ground when Louis just happened to look back. "Kick um out! Trouble is on our tails!"

Those horses leaped into an all out run as all four men pulled their pistols, firing at the on coming riders. Randy's horse went down instantly just as Travis was got shot high in the left shoulder.

Casey grabbed his reins and slowed the horses. "Darn it Travis, we knew better than that!"

"Yeah, shor do now anyhow. Let's get back an' see if Randy made it."

"How bad are you got? Looks like that slug just cut meat pretty good."

"It shor do hurt, but nothin' like our ears will when we get home. Mom is going to have a screamin' fit."

"Yep, 'spect she will. I'll take care of the horses and stay out of the house until she has to take break from screamin."

"Oh she'll get around to you even if she has to walk out to the barn."

They got back to Randy and he was sitting up with a broken arm. "Boy howdy Gus is shor gonna be mad me gettin' that horse killed. You got bad, Travis?"

"Good enough that I won't be catchin' them suckers for ah while. Get up behind Casey an' we'll head back for the house. Dad and Casey can come for yore saddle an' gear. Mom'll fix us both up. Just you keep yore mouth shut when she starts screaming. Only utter the words like yes ma'am and no ma'am and we just might come out of this alive."

Just walking the horses, it took them a good while making that two and a half miles back to the house. Joel was just walking around the side of the barn and stopped dead still for just a moment.

Then he walked over and helped Randy down and Casey stepped down. Joel said, "From the looks of you two I'd say you ran into those ol' boys a lot quicker than you thought you would."

Casey held Travis's horse as he stepped from the saddle. "I'll water and tie the horses, y'all go on in."

Travis turned and smiled, "Coward."

Joel opened the door and Travis walked in first, Randy then Joel. Tiny looked up from the stove and saw Travis's bloody shoulder. She pulled out a chair, "Sit, let me take a look at that."

Travis sat and Tiny looked at Randy. "That means you too, sit!"

Joel was getting a pan of hot water and rags as Tiny took Travis's shirt off. "My goodness, now that is a nasty hole. Joel while I clean this up, get my needle and thread, oh and that tin of wool fat."

As she worked on that shoulder she just had to ask, "How dumb were you this time? Is Casey all right, I don't see he came in with you."

"Casey's fine, just a little coward."

"He has a right to be. I have no idea what happened, but trying to pull something stupid is all I can think of."

"It was, caught sight of those robbers just as we got to the stage road. We got a bit too close."

"And you both know not to chase gunmen. You or your horse will get killed."

"Yeah, Randy's horse was killed right off."

"Poor thing, I'm sorry to hear that."

She patted Travis just as she put his arm in a sling. "You'll be just fine now to look at that crooked arm of Randy's."

He asked, "You ever take care of a broken arm before?"

"Joel twice, Travis once and Casey twice. Yep, I'm an old hand at it. Oh, and my own ankle twice."

She rolled up his sleeve and just above that left wrist Tiny could tell it really was broken. "Joel, come here."

Joel walked over and grinned, "Yep, hang on to his elbow and I'll give that a yank."

Randy almost passed out, but looked at that arm and it was straight. "Darn, looks good."

Tiny said, "I'll have to wrap it tight then we'll take you in to the doctor so he can put it in a cast."

"Joel said we!"

"Yes, we'll have to stop by his horse and get his saddle and bridle. There's nothing Travis can't do one handed and get the chores done. We'll have to stay the night in town."

Travis asked, 'What about Casey?"

"Now that's a dumb question. He going after those men. Not only for robbing that bank but for shooting that horse and you."

"You mean he'll go alone!"

"You're certainly not going with him! That shoulder has to be looked after."

She walked to the door and hollered, "Casey, what's taking you so long?"

"Be right there, Mama."

He walked in, with a weak smile. "Yes Mama?"

Tiny looked at him. "Casey Pascoe you ever pull another stunt like that if it doesn't kill you, I just might! What in the world were you thinking?"

"Wasn't I don't guess."

"Think you can get those fellows?"

"Yeah, it'll take a good while being as I'll have to wait 'til I catch um in some town where I can get law and plenty of help."

"Then I'd say you'd better get a move on. You don't think they're just sitting out there waiting, do you?"

"No mama. I get a chance I'll sent Gus a telegram ever now and ah gain an' let y'all know where I am."

He started for the door, Tiny said, "I love you Casey, just you be mighty careful. Travis won't be with you to lend a hand this time."

"Yeah, an' most likely I'll need him. Bye y'all."

He got his horse and rode northeast saving a few miles getting to that stage road. He knew four sets of tracks would be easy to follow.

CHAPTER TWO

A short bit before sundown Casey rode up to the Longhorn stage stop that was right on top of a hill. He could see for miles on east and almost to his house southwest. He stopped at the livery and stepped down just as the west bound stage came to a stop in a cloud of dust.

Casey asked the hostler, "Will you still have room for my horse?"

"Shor do young fellow. Get him watered, it'll be a bit 'fore them boys drive that stage on over here to unhitch the horses. They'll have some unloading to do first. Yep, looks like four passengers. Say, one of um's looker! Mighty pretty gal, that one."

Casey smiled, "See even at yore age you can still spot um. Wonder if that one is all stuck up."

"Some of the pretty ones are alright, some ain't. Guess we'll see at the supper table."

As they took care of the horse, Casey didn't see a red and white paint. "Say, did four fellers stop by here, one ridin' a red an' white paint?"

"Shor nuff did, rode out over three hours ah go. Said they wanted to make it to Santa Rosa by night tomorrow. Horses looked to be pretty much wore out. They'd better ride slow er stop an' rest um ever twenty miles er so. Course they'll stop for the night anytime now, I'd think."

They walked out front just as four cowboys rode up. The hostler shook his head, "Damn, that's all we need, that damn bunch of trouble makers."

"Who er they?"

"Wallace cowboys an' old man Wallace ain't with um so after a few drinks in that saloon they'll get into fights and bust the place up."

Casey said, "If it was my place they wouldn't. I'd pull ah double barrel shotgun from behind that bar. One dime's worth of damage they'd pay."

He looked at Casey and smiled, "Shor like yore way ah thinkin', young feller. You may's well go on an' have ah beer while me an them two Overland Stage boys takes care of them four horses."

Casey walked in and the huge bar was on the right, dining room on the left and hotel straight ahead. Those four Wallace cowboys already had them a bottle and were sitting at a close table.

Casey stopped at the bar and ordered a beer. With that in his left hand, he turned and looked those four cowboys over, then lifted his eyes to the dining room. Four people, one was that pretty girl and a women Casey figgered the mother, one of the men the father as they were all sitting close at the table. An older man sat alone three chairs down.

Casey sniffed the air and smiled, food! "Man, does that ever smell good, didn't know I's so hungry."

The hostler, stage driver and guard walked in and into the dining room. As they sat, Casey set his empty beer mug and headed that way.

He sat directly across from the driver and guard as food was already on the table, everyone started passing around platters of meat, potatoes, gravy and biscuits.

As they ate, the folks talked of the long trip and where they were going. Casey asked about how far back they saw four riders. The driver looked at the Guard asking, "What do you think, Tom? Fifteen er so miles? Ought'a be better'n thirty by now."

"Then they'll make Santa Rosa tomorrow, I'd guess."

"Yeah, ought'a, easy. You headed that'a way?"

"Yes Sir, shor do need to catch up with um."

"Kind'a gettin' ah late start, ain't ya?"

"Yeah, reckon, but I've got ah while. Might just get um 'fore they get to Arkansas. That is if I can gain a little ground ever day."

Both said at the same time, "Arkansas!"

The driver asked, "Why Arkansas?"

"They robbed the bank in Bernalillo then shot my brother and a deputy's horse."

"Now hold on boy, yer too dad gum young to be law. Best you leave that up to them."

"Yep, and they'd never be caught. Naw, I'll get um. It'll take ah while, as I'll take my time."

"You've either got guts er yer dumb to the core."

"What would either of you do it they'd shot yore brother?"

"Go after um… Oh, guess you are."

That young girl and her parents had been listening and the girl asked, "Does your mother know?"

"Yep, she insisted."

The old man that was sitting alone said, "Son, do it right and stay alive. Guess you know a wounded man can kill you. Don't give them no more of a chance than they'd give you. Got a few bullet holes in me from thinking a fellow was dead, before he was."

Casey said, "You sound like law."

"Was, years back. Got too old and ran out of speed. Knew about any gunnie out there could outdraw me. I just quit while I'm still alive."

Casey smiled, "Glad you made it."

"Son, I'd sure like to buy you a beer and bend your ear, if you don't mind."

"Thanks, but I'll buy." They both asked to be excused, got up and walked over to the bar.

Casey said, "Take that table, I'll get the beer."

They sat and talked and a bit later that girl and her parents walked from the dining room, headed for their room. One of those Wallace cowboys jumped up and ran over blocking them.

"Now why don't you folks just come over and sit awhile? We'll have us ah drink where I can get to know this pretty little girl."

The man said, "Please excuse us sir, and thank you but we do not drink."

"Then by damn it's about time you started!"

As he grabbed that girl by the arm, that father knocked the hell out of him. He staggered back, but before he could swing back, Casey had hold of that arm.

"Think these..." Three more men headed that way.

Casey turned the fellow's arm loose and stood between that cowboy and those folks. "Best you call it quits. These folks want to be left alone."

"Cowboy, stickin' yore nose where it don't belong can get it broke."

That old man sitting at the table pulled and cocked a forty-four. "Boys, those folks want to be left alone. And just one of you hurt my little friend, it'll make me awful mad. None of you really want to see me get mad, now do you?"

"Now look here old man…"

That pistol pointed where every one of them knew he wouldn't miss. One said, "What the hell, didn't want'a buy um a drink no how!"

They all four backed off and went back to their table. The father of that girl thanked Casey and that old man, then hurried on toward their room.

The driver and guard had seen this and both confronted those Wallace cowboys. "You boys ever touch another of our passengers, Henry will damn shor hear about it!"

"We's just funnin'. Won't happen again."

"That's what I like to hear." They turned walked back to Casey's table, "Mind if we sit?"

"Pull out ah chair."

The next morning Casey rode out before sunup. He knew if he really pushed his horse, he'd make Santa Rosa well after sundown. Three hours later he came upon the pond where the Lees and Morgans had camped for the night.

After watering his horse, he pushed on. "Don't remember the law they've got in Santa Rosa, shor do hope he's ah good un. I mean if I do run into them ol' boys this quick. Now wouldn't that be something."

Well before Casey rode off that long hill headed toward the Pecos River and Santa Rosa, the Morgans and Lees were in the saloon drinking and playing poker. Out front all the hitch rails had been full, so they tied their horses around back with over a dozen more. With cinches loosened, they looked around at that vacant lot with ten hitchrails far enough apart strange horses couldn't fight and kick each other. Before walking in that back door, Louis had told all of them, no damn trouble. "We drink, play poker then get some sleep."

Reese said, "After I have one drink, I'm gonna get me ah woman."

"You do that, but don't you rough her up. Pay and keep yore mouth shut. She comes out'a that room bawlin', you've got me to deal with, not law."

"Now darn it Louis, you know the one I kicked the hell out of tried stealin' my money."

"You didn't have to break her jaw! That was right down stupid dumb. Yore fine was a hundred dollars. Could have been jail time."

"Hell, only hit her twice."

"This one not once, hear me."

Casey slowly rode into town, looking but knew he wouldn't see that paint horse. Just as he was riding past the sheriff's office, the sheriff stepped out of that office headed to the saloon for one drink before going home for the night.

"Howdy Sheriff, got ah minute."

"Yep, what do you have on your mind?"

The sheriff listened and eyeballed Casey. "Son, do you expect me to believe that sheriff sent a kid after bank robbers? Did he deputize you?"

"No, I'm a bounty hunter, of sorts. My brother was with me until he got shot right off. I took him home."

The sheriff let a small smile come to his lips. "Get that horse took care of, I'll be in the saloon."

After unsaddling his horse, Casey looked every horse in there over and even looked at those in the back lot. He headed for the saloon.

Just before he walked in, Lindal said, "Damn Louis, we forgot an' left them horses standin'. We need to get um to the livery an' fed er they won't be worth ah damn tomorrow."

"I'll finish this hand an' we'll do that. Time for bed anyhow."

Casey walked in the front door and saw the sheriff. As he walked over and stood beside him, the sheriff ordered him a beer.' Casey took it in his left hand saying. "They must have just rode on thru. I didn't see their horses in the livery."

The sheriff took a long drink of beer, wiped his mouth and said, "They might'a just tied um around back if them hitchrails out front was full. That lot back there'll hold another twenty horses. Finish yore beer an' we'll go take ah look."

Just before Casey and the sheriff finished their beers and set the mugs down, the Morgans and Lees had walked out that back door. Casey and the sheriff no more than a minute behind.

With that full moon shining brightly, it was easy to see all those horses and several men getting ready to mount. It just wasn't bright enough to make out what the men looked like.

As the Morgans and Lees tightened cinches and stepped into their saddles, Casey saw that paint. "That's them Sheriff! Right there riding off!"

Like a dummy, that sheriff hollered out, "You men! Hold it right there!"

Casey had already dived to the ground pulling his forty-five as the sheriff was knocked down. On his belly the sheriff grabbed his forty-four and knocked Charlie from his saddle, Casey got Reese but Louis and Lindal were laying over their saddle horns and moved thru those other horses then around a building and onto the street. Neither Casey or the sheriff could get off another shot.

The Sheriff hollered out, "You check them two out, boy. One of um moves you put a slug in him before he can pull ah trigger."

As Casey walked forward, finger on that hammer. Men poured out the back door of the saloon wondering what all the shooting was about.

The sheriff heard them and shouted, "Don't none of y'all shoot! I'm down but so is two of the shooters.

Got ah cowboy checkin' um now. Come give me ah hand up. If they're alive I'll need help gettin' um to jail."

Casey eased up and kicked a gun from Reese's hand then walked over and did the same to Charlie. He called out to the sheriff, "Both of um's still alive, out cold. Don't know for how long if they ain't got to ah doc. How bad er you hit?"

"About enough to know how stupid I was hollering out like that. Got me in the left thigh. Didn't hit no bone."

"How can you tell?"

"Got two holes bleedin' like heck. Need a couple of y'all to stuff bandannas in um 'til I get to the doc."

Louis and Lindal had slowed their horses as soon as they were on the street. Louis said, "Damn, with no telegraph over this'a way, I wonder how in the hell he got word even 'fore we got here."

"We gonna somehow check an' see if Charlie and Reese is gonna make er if they're both dead?"

"Hell, ain't nothin' we can do alive er dead. They'll just have to take their chances. Glad I kept that bank bag stuffed in my shirt."

"We still goin' to grandpas?"

"Hell yes, plumb out'a New Mexico. Just glad neither of our horses was hit. They'll not know which way we went. We'll ride up river a fair piece an' get some shut eye. Ridin' out before sunup, we'll come to ah stage stop well before noon an' eat ah bite. Reese had most of the grub. I just have ah couple cans ah beans and coffee. What have you got."

"Jerky an' coffee's about it."

As they unsaddled and rolled out bedrolls, the doctor had bandaged the sheriff and was looking at Reese and Charlie. Casey asked what he thought.

"Both have more than a fair chance. Worse was being knocked out when they hit that hard ground wrong. Don't feel like they have broken necks and neither lost much blood. Sheriff, you ready for me to bring them to? I have those slugs out. One from a forty-four the other is a forty-five."

"Bring um to, they can't get to no gun where I'd really have to shoot um."

He reached back for a bottle of smelling salts and gave Reese a whiff first. His eyes popped open, "What the hell happened?"

"You got shot from your horse."

"Oh yeah, who was shootin' at us."

"That sheriff sitting right there with that mad look. You see, one of you also shot him. That's why he's mad. Watch this." He gave Charlie a whiff out of that bottle and he sat straight up, looking around.

"How'd I get here?"

"Yer shot, just not good enough! Now where did yore two friends get off to?"

He laughed, "Don't worry sheriff, they'll find you. You don't think they'd run off an' leave us, do you?"

"Then you have that bank money on you?"

"No."

"Then boy, yer left. Those two just have two less to split all that money with."

"Naw… Reese, you think…?"

"Sheriff's right, they don't know if we're dead er not. We've seen the last of um."

Casey said, "Now hold on there. I'll get um either alive er dead. If that teller died, maybe y'all can hang together, 'less I have to kill um. They'll be jumpy as all get out for ah few days."

"Who'n the hell are you?"

"The brother of the fellow you shot over this side of Albuquerque. Same time you shot an' killed that deputy's horse."

"You! You follered us all this way!"

"I did and if I have to, I'll foller them two all the way to their grandpa Lee's in Arkansas. I even know where he lives out on Burnt Stump Road."

"How'n the hell did you know all of that an' where we's goin'?"

"It seems as their grandmother Hodges didn't know she had two outlaws as grandsons. We even got to see pictures of all four of y'all. Took last July it says. She was willing to share."

"You mean that old woman went against own blood kin! Hell of ah grandma she is!"

Casey smiled, "I'd say quite to woman. She even knows right from wrong."

"Go to hell!"

"Don't save me ah seat, you'll beat me there."

"Like hell! We ain't hung yet. You don't even got us back to Bernalillo, yet. Can't do it by yore self, boy. I'll get to wring yore damn neck."

"Well ol' buddy boy, I guess you just don't know Casey Pascoe."

"Who in the hell's that?"

"Me." He laughed. "Sheriff I'm headed for bed. Can them two be kept 'till I can get back thru here?"

"They well be, but if you'll share some of that reward, I'll send as much help with you, you think you'll need when you come an' get um. Two prisoners, take one other man. Four prisoners, take two extra men. You'll get um there."

"Now that sounds like it'll work. Save me having to shoot um when they try to escape. As I said, I'm headed for me ah bed. After all, y'all know I'm just ah growin' boy that needs his rest."

The next morning Casey ate breakfast as soon as the café opened and was riding east before sunup.

Lindal and Louis had already been riding for over an hour. Lindal asked, "Don't they have stage stops ever thirty er forty miles?"

"Ought'a least be one before Liberty. Then it's all the way over in Texas at Tascosa. Now I heard one time that place you darn shor want'a stay out'a trouble in. Gobs of fellers on the run from all over Texas hang out there. Oh yeah, an XIT cowboys. You mess with them... Well we won't that's all I can say."

"What about that place you called Liberty?"

"Small cow town, mostly used by the Bell Ranch cowboys. Ought'a not be no law."

(Liberty) Three miles north of modern-day Tucumcari, New Mexico.

Before noon they rode up to the stage stop called Lone Mountain Stage Station. A small clear running creek is where horses were watered. They rode up, dismounted and tied the horses.

"Man, smellin' that grub makes my guts growl. Must be cookin' for the next stage."

"Yeah, if so, it'll be along shortly. Let's eat and get. I want to make Liberty by dark, if we can."

Casey was coming on strong and had picked up several miles. Now he was only an hour behind.

CHAPTER THREE

Louis and Lindal walked in the stage stop and ordered coffee and a big meal. As they ate, Louis asked, "Why's this called Lone Mountain?"

The fellow looked at him saying, "Cause of that lone mountain right out yonder."

"You call that a mountain! You ought'a go west to the Rockies if you want'a see ah mountain."

"Son, in this low rollin' hill country any pile of dirt an' rocks over ah hundred feet tall's called a mountain. That one is right at three hundred feet."

Louis laughed, "Lone Mountain it is. Think we can make Liberty 'fore night?"

"Could if you get ah move on. Be sundown anyhow. Grady closes his livery half hour after sundown. That's right at dark."

They rode out a half hour later and did kick the horses into a good fast gallop. Lindal said he hoped Reese and Charlie made it. Louis grinned, "Yeah, a few years in prison beats bein' dead all to hell."

Lindal looked over at him, "Yeah, we've got all that money an' they'll go to prison for us."

Louis laughed, "Yeah, good boys them Morgans all ways was. We'll have ah drink to um ever now and ah gain just for the hell of it."

"Wonder if they'll tell we're headed for grandpas."

"Naw, they'd never do that. They ain't dead they'll keep their mouths shut. Well, if they's dead they will too, I reckon." He laughed and patted that bank money that was still stuffed in his shirt.

They met the west bound stage two miles later and got off the road so they wouldn't get run over. That driver was using his whip and had those horses in a run. "Knows he's gonna be late for dinner."

"Yeah, er he's gotta use that outhouse."

Casey rode up the stage stop, dismounted and loosened the saddle cinch. That stage pulled to a dusty stop. Passengers stepped down, dusting off their clothes before walking inside. Horses were watered then the driver and guard followed Casey thru that door.

The meal was a noisy one as everyone had something to talk about. Casey listened, ate in a hurry and went for his horse. As he rode out, he talked to his horse.

"Shor do wish Travis was along. Horse, don't you let me ride into trouble. Could you know. Travis is the one that most times saw trouble comin. Yeah, an' boy howdy mama shor would get mad at me if I went an' got myself shot."

Louis and Lindal rode into Liberty just at sundown. As they stalled the horses making sure they were well fed, Lindal asked the hostler if this was Saturday.

"Naw, Friday, why?"

"All them horses tied around that saloon."

"That's the Bell Ranch cowboys and a few of Donald Gentry's. They cause no trouble... Well some now and ah gain if they drink ah dab too much. They'll get to arguing about who's horse is the fastest. Then they'll walk out an' get their horses an' have um a horse race. Then they'll have one hell of ah fight because one er the other cheated."

"Do they cheat?"

"Hell no, but one of um'll lose and just knows his horse should'a won. He gets mad, fist will fly."

"We ain't gonna get in no horse race. We've come darn near sixty miles today. A couple drinks an' grub's all we're after."

"Then don't get in no poker game, that can come to guns if there's ah big loser."

"We'll go eat then have us ah drink."

They had been gone from the livery a good bit when Casey rode in on a tired horse. Unsaddling and feeding that tired horse, he saw in the next stall that red and white paint.

He threw his saddle over the partition and reached down taking the tie down off the hammer of his forty-five. The hostler saw that and smiled. "Smart boy."

"Huh?" Casey was thinking how he was going to take those two without getting a few cowboys shot.

"I said smart, takin' that tie down off while you had time. If needed, it'd been too late."

"Yeah, seen ah few fellers shot slappin' leather with their gun still tied down."

Casey walked on over to the café and ate a good meal, still wondering how he should handle this. "Maybe I ought'a wait 'til they go for their horses in the mornin'."

The waitress smiled, "Kind'a young to be talking to yourself."

Casey looked up and also smiled. "Yeah, searching for answers an' found none. Just don't want'a do something stupid that could get me killed. Do y'all got any law around here?"

"No, but Marshal Billingsley is over at the saloon. He's from up at Raton. He followed a horse thief all this way and got him."

"Where's his horse thief now?"

"In lock up over at the feed store. It has a storeroom that no one can get out of. Only has one small window up high. He couldn't get out that even if he could climb up there."

Casey ate then slowly walked toward the saloon. "Well, for shor they don't know me, but I'll darn shor know them."

He walked in and stopped at the bar ordering a beer. Looking around, he was hoping to see that marshal, but no one he saw was wearing a badge.

Just to the left of that hallway and back door sat Lindal and Louis with a bottle in front of them. Casey finished his beer, watching and thinking. He knew when confronted they'd both go for their guns and some of these cowboys would take lead, or him.

"If I can come in that back door and get the drop on them... Yeah, that ought'a work an' maybe I could lock um in that feed storeroom for the night."

He walked out the front door and all the way around back. He looked at the two outhouses, but heard nothing.

Slowly walking in, that hallway was short, past two rooms, one on the left, one on the right then the saloon. He stopped, and could see both men not six feet way. No one was paying any attention, so he slowly pulled his forty-five and eased forward. Just before he got there, he was slammed in back of the head and fell forward right on Lindal's back, spilling his drink. Lindal jumped up as Casey fell flat of his face in the floor.

There stood Marshal Billingsley, with his pistol in his hand. "What the hell!" Lindal and Louis both had their hands on the butts of their pistols.

"That kid was just about to shoot y'all in the back."

Lindal reached down turning Casey face up. "Hell, I've never seen him before."

The marshal smiled, "Maybe not, but I'd say he's seen y'all. Best y'all give me ah hand. We'll take him down and lock him in that feed storeroom."

He picked Casey's pistol up and handed it to the bartender. "Give it back to him in a couple days. I'll tell the store owner to feed him and maybe two days he'll cool off. Might'a just been drunk."

"Yeah, we won't be here. We're just ridin' thru." Louis said as he really took a good look at Casey.

They picked him up and ten minutes later Casey was laid out on a bunch of feed sacks. The marshal looked at his prisoner. "Bruce, get yore sleep. We'll be leaving right after breakfast."

Walking back to the saloon, the bartender talked with the marshal. "Marshal, I don't think that kid was drunk. He only drank one beer then walked out."

"Well for fact if I hadn't gone to the outhouse an' walked back in when I did, I'd say them two fellows would'a been back shot."

"That's being called at the right place, right time. Saved two killings."

Lindal and Louis was at their table and Lindal picked up his glass that was still on the floor. Pouring drinks Louis said, "I shor's hell can't figger what that was all about. Stupid kid."

"Yeah, we know damn well we've never seen him. Maybe he just wants to make ah name for his self where he could brag, he'd killed ah couple fellers."

"I ain't gonna think no more on it. We'll ride before sunup."

The next morning Lindal and Louis was at the café when it opened. That marshal walked on over to the feed store to get his prisoner. The owner had walked in the back door and was standing at the stove getting a cup of coffee.

"Well Marshal, guess y'all will eat and ride."

"Yeah, here's your door key. I put a young fellow in there last night that was just about to back shoot a couple fellows. When me an' Bruce eats breakfast, I'll have the cook bring him something."

They walked over and removed that two by six that had that door wedged shut. Opening the door he said, "Come on Bruce, breakfast is waitin."

A Bruce walked out, he said, "You know Marshal, that kid never moved one time last night. Still hadn't"

"What?" He stepped in looking at Casey, exactly as he was when they laid him there.

"Damn, I might'a killed that kid, hittin' him harder than I meant to."

He walked over and felt Casey's chest. "Naw, he's alive, strong heart beat and breath."

He turned to the store owner, "Guess y'all don't got no doctor. He might need one."

"Naw, after I have my coffee, I'll walk over and see if Mrs. Sewell will come take a look at him. She does most of our doctoring."

"Thanks, you do that." He and Bruce walked out and to the café.

Lindal and Louis had just finished breakfast and were ready to leave. "How's that little cowboy this mornin'?" Lindal asked with a smile.

"Not too good, he's still out."

"Boy howdy you must'a knocked the hell plumb out'a him."

"Harder than I thought anyhow."

Louis said, "Thanks again Marshal. At least somebody ain't havin' to dig two graves this mornin."

They got their horses and headed for Tascosa. The marshal and Bruce ate then went to the livery for their horses. The hostler said, "A little cowboy left his horse here last night. Must'a been really tired, he hadn't come for him yet."

"Nice lookin' young cowboy, early twenties?"

"Yeah, you seen him?"

"I have, it'll be a couple days 'fore he comes for his horse. He's in y'all's lock up."

"Dad gum, shor didn't seem the type to cause no trouble."

"He was gettin' ready to back shoot ah couple fellers when I stopped him."

"Naw! Boy howdy I wouldn't ah thunk it."

The Marshal and Bruce rode out headed north and would cross the Canadian River by noon, on their way to Raton. They had over a hundred miles to go.

The store owner was in no hurry, having two cups of coffee. He looked in on Casey, "Still sleeping, best I get over and eat breakfast then check with Mrs. Sewell.

She'll have her breakfast dishes washed an' put away by then. She won't mind checkin' the boy."

It was almost an hour before Mrs. Sewell looked in on Casey. "Good Lord! Who in the world did this to this boy?"

"Marshal Billingsley out of Raton done it last night."

"Get me water heated, I'll have to step back over to the house for my bandages. Why in the world didn't you come get me as soon as you saw this boy?"

"Now Maude, you know I ain't any blamed good in the morning until after I have my coffee. Yeah, and I had to eat breakfast. You know how weak I get if I don't eat."

"Ross, you and that marshal both need to be horse whipped! I cannot believe just how stupid some men are. I'll be right back."

She got back with bandages and wrapping and said, "Now hand me a pan of hot water."

With one of her clean rags, she washed and bathed that open wound. Then she put gobs of wool fat on it and bandaged his head, wrapping the bandage completely around.

"Alright go to the well and bring me a bucket of water."

"I have water right here."

"The well! I need the coldest we have."

"Yes Maude, the well."

With that cold water she bathed Cassey's face, neck and chest. Over and over again she wet that rag. Casey stirred, opened his eyes and tried to smile looking into the eyes of a woman.

"Howdy Ma'am."

"And hello to you, young man. You gave me a worry there for a while."

"Any idea who clobbered me?"

"Yes, a marshal."

"Marshal! Why in the world?"

"Ross said you were about to shoot two men in the back over at the saloon."

"Dog gone it, I wadn't gonna shoot um. I was going to take them back to Bernalillo where they could be tried for bank robbery."

Ross said, "Bank robbers!"

"Yes, bank robbers." Casey sat up, slowly. "They also shot my brother and shot and killed a deputy's horse. I guess the marshal and both of those men have gone."

"Yes, hours ago."

"I need to get me something to eat and get after them as quick as I can."

"Young man, you take it from an old woman. You are not fit to be riding a horse. You could have dizzy spells and fall off and kill yourself. You need Ross to help you over to my house and you rest up for today. We'll see how you feel in the morning."

"Boy howdy this most likely mean's I'll have to go all the way to Arkansas to catch them now."

"Arkansas!"

"Yes Ma'am, thanks to that marshal. I just hope one day I get to return the favor."

"Now hold on son, he just…" Ross looked at him.

"Instead of trying to kill me, he could have stuck that pistol in my back. Of course, then we'd both most likely been shot."

Maude asked, "With Ross's help think you could make it a half block?"

"If you'll feed me breakfast I'll shor give it ah try."

"I sure can do that. Ross, give him a hand."

Casey stood and did have to grab hold of Ross. His head was swimming and he couldn't focus his eyes.

Maude quickly handed him a cup of that cold water. "Try this, see if it helps. I'd hate to leave you lying here on these feed sacks all day."

He sat back down and drink two cups of water and his head seemed to clear just a bit. Handing her the cup he said, "I'm ready to give it a try."

With Ross's help, Casey made it alright. "Just sit right there at the table. I'll fix your breakfast. Thanks Ross, for your help."

Ross left and Maude set a cup of coffee in front of Casey. She looked at him, "Well, I see you're getting some of your color back."

"Yeah, feel pretty good right now. Not dizzy at all."

"After a good breakfast you'll feel even better."

All morning Casey sat on the porch looking over the small town. Maude called him into dinner and they ate. "Well Casey, you have all of your color."

"Yep, I feel about like my old self."

"Now I want you to go back and lie down for at least an hour. When you get up, I'll clean that wound and see how it looks."

"I can feel some of the swelling has gone down."

"Then let me take that bandage off now and you keep a cold wet rag on it while you nap."

She walked around and removed the bandage. "My goodness, it sure does look much better."

She wet a rag and handed it to him. "Now get, nap and you'll feel even better."

About two o'clock Casey walked out on the porch to find Maude reading. "Feel better. Think I'll leave that bandage off an' let some air get to it."

"It's your head, whatever you think."

"Say meant to asked, have you seen my forty-five?"

"No, maybe it fell out of your holster in that feed room. Or even the bartender might have it."

"Yeah, bet that's where it is 'cause I had it in my hand when that marshal clobbered me. After a bit I'll walk over to the saloon a' see an' might even have me a beer."

"Now that might do you some good. No chance of getting hit again, that marshal has gone."

"Lucky him." Casey grinned.

Around five Casey said he'd go on over to the saloon for his pistol and have a beer.

Maude said, "Now don't be long, supper will be ready in about an' hour."

She reached inside the door and got his hat. "See if you can wear that."

Casey put it on. "Yeah, a little lop-sided but it'll do."

Casey walked in the saloon and stopped at the bar. The bartender looked at him and smiled. Reaching under the bar, he got Casey's pistol and handed it to him. "I guess it'll be a while before you try shooting anyone else in the back."

Casey looked at him and snapped. "I shor as hell wasn't tryin' to shoot them two in the back. And that stupid marshal just let two bank robbers get away."

"He what? Naw!"

"Yeah, I'd follered um all the way from Bernalillo. Now it looks like it'll be all the way to Russellville Arkansas before I get um now. There was four of um, but was able with help get two of um in Santa Rosa. Least that sheriff was a help. I need ah beer."

The bartender drew the beer and set if in front of Casey. "On the house, cowboy. Maude treating you alright, looks like."

"Nice lady, reminds me of my grandma Bartie."

Casey finished the beer and headed on back to Maude's. As they ate supper Casey said he'd be riding out after breakfast.

"You seem to feel up to it."

As they talked, Louis and Lindal was in Tascosa right in the middle of a poker game. Louis had already told Lindal as sorry as these cowboys played poker, they just might stay over a day or two.

Lindal had answered by saying, "No, darn it we need to be movin' on. We've got plenty ah money."

"Yeah, but them boys are easy an' we don't gotta use our guns to get it."

CHAPTER FOUR

The next morning Casey and Maude were eating breakfast early. Maude knew he wanted to leave as soon as possible. Casey asked, "Can I have one last cup of that good coffee?"

She smiled, got up and walked to the stove for the coffee pot. Casey slipped a ten-dollar gold piece under his plate he knew she'd see it as soon as she picked that plate up.

He downed that coffee, got up saying, "Maude you'll never know how much I thank you for taking care of me. You an' my grandma Bartie sure would make a pair. She's the goodest."

"Ahh go on now. I'd done it for anyone in need."

She walked with him to the door telling him to take care of himself. He hurried off as Maude went back to the table. "I sure enjoyed that little rascal."

She picked up his plate and saw that ten-dollar gold piece. She ran to the door, jerked it open and yelled, "Casey Pascoe you come back here and I'll really put another knot on your head!"

Casey heard that and laughed. Walking in the livery the hostler eyeballed him pretty good. "Guess that marshal taught you not to try an' back shoot anybody when he's around."

"Well Grady, I sure wasn't trying to back shoot no body. I was trying to grab two bank robbers. All that marshal did was help them get away. Does anybody around here have one brain cell in their heads? Just how stupid do they think I am to walk right up behind somebody and back shoot him when I could have done it from that back door and not been seen."

"Huh? Never thought ah that. Yeah, come to think on it I'd used the back door an' run like hell, not get clubbed in the head."

Casey paid for his horse being stalled and rode out for Tascosa just at sunup. Pushing hard he knew he could make it before sundown.

Two hours later, Louis and Lindal rode east, southeast from Tascosa. By pushing hard, they would easily make the railroad, cattle town of Amarillo well before sundown. As they loped along, Louis said, "What'd I tell you about them dumb cowboys? Not a one of um knowed how to play poker. Made us over two hundred dollars."

"Yeah, but we could'a already been leavin' Amarillo right now 'stead of Tascosa."

"What the hell's yore hurry? All we'll do when we get to grandpas is fish, an' lay around gettin' drunk."

"That's just it Louis, now that we've got money we drink too damn much. One day it'll get us in trouble."

Louis laughed, "Hell, we know how to get out'a trouble. Just go rob us ah bank. Yeah, an' down in Arkansas they don't use stage coaches no more so maybe we'll have to try robbin' us ah train. I mean if we ever run out'a money."

"I ain't robbin' no train! Just get that out'a yore head! Banks yeah, trains hell no."

"Now hold on, Lindal. I heared way back them James' boys done alright robbin' trains."

"We're darn shor not the James boys by a long shot. They had ten er twelve men helpin' them. Yeah, an' knowed what they was doin'. We wouldn't know jack squat about the first thing robbin' trains. Farther more, I don't want'a learn."

"Get hungry enough boy, you'll learn in ah hurry."

They rode into Amarillo and didn't even take care of the horses as they stopped at the Cattlemen's Saloon and Hotel. Louis said, "Drink before food is always best, er is it the other way round? Naw, it's drink." He laughed and after tying the horses in a vacant lot with other horses and buggies, they walked into that very fancy saloon.

The doorman stopped them. "May I help you gentlemen?"

"If yer the bartender, yeah. We need a drink."

The door man smiled, "Sir, this is a gentlemen's club. Working cowboys cannot afford the price of our drinks."

"The hell you say! Then where can a poor workin' boy get his self ah drink er two?"

"Any of the other half dozen saloons. The tent saloons are the cheapest, whiskey a nickel, beer a dime. But you know most of those still have dirt floors."

"And what do y'all get here?"

"Whiskey a quarter, and mug of beer a half dollar. You see a cowboy would run out of money pretty quick. Two drinks a day's wages gone."

"In other words, whoever owns this place is a damn crook? Come on Lindal, they couldn't pay me enough to spend one… quarter in there."

They walked for their horses and Lindal said, "What the hell, we've got the money."

"Yeah, but I hate a damn crook. His whiskey an' beer ain't no better than anybody else's."

They got their horses and rode on up the street. "Yeah, an' bet his girls is stuck up to. Maybe even ah dollar 'stead of ah quarter er even fifty cents."

They stopped in front of the Plains Saloon where a few horses were tied out front. Walking in, Louis looked for a door man and smiled when there wasn't one. They walked to the bar and bellowed out, "Whiskey!"

The bartender asked, "Glass er bottle?"

"Glass, we'll be back after we stall the horses an' get us ah bottle. Have to get rid of trail dust first."

The bartender brought the drinks, "That'll be ah dime."

Louis laid a quarter on the bar, "Keep it, this is good whiskey."

"Thanks Cowboy!"

They downed that drink and asked where the livery is. "Three blocks north, just to the east of the train depot. He'll have to move it 'fore long, train noise."

"Yeah, bet that does scare the hell out'a horses. That hotel across the street a good un?"

"Yeah, Swede keeps it mighty clean."

They took care of the horses, got a room and were back in the saloon in less than an hour.

Casey rode into Tascosa just after sundown and as he took his horse into the livery, a gunfight broke out up the street. The hostler said, "Knowed that was gonna happen. Hope they kill each other off."

"Know who it is?"

"Yeah, two different bunches ah gunnies rode in a few hours ah go. Been in that saloon just long enough to get drunk. Folks better drop behind something, them skunks don't care who they..."

A shotgun blast was heard loud and clear. "Sounds like Sheriff Bennett might'a got ah few of um."

More gunshots, then all was quiet. Casey unsaddled and took care of his horse while asking about a red and white paint horse.

"Yes sir, mighty fine looking animal he was. They rode out pretty early this morning. Eight I'd say."

"This morning! Damn, I thought I's two days er better behind them."

"Would'a been but they got in a high dollar poker game for two nights. Don't know if they won er lost but they did pay for their horse's keep with no griping. Headed southeast toward Amarillo."

"Dang if that's not ah stroke ah luck. Now I'm just one day back. Who knows, maybe I can still catch um 'fore they get to Arkansas."

They both walked out front and looked up the street. "That's Sheriff Bennett looking at those three bodies. Looks like them other fellers high tailed it."

"I'm gonna eat then get a beer. Bet that whole saloon will be talkin' about that shootin'."

"Spect they will an' each one'll have a good excuse why they wadn't out there helping the sheriff."

Casey ate then walked over to the saloon. He just wanted to sit and quietly drink his beer.

He had almost finished that one and was thinking of one more then going to bed early. In the door walked the sheriff and two men. They stopped half way down the bar and the bartender set beers in front of them.

The sheriff was facing the back of the room, talking to two fellows that asked who the dead men were. "Strangers, all three of um. They sure put some bullet holes in buildings trying to kill each other. No telling what that gunfight was about."

All of a sudden out of that chair Casey came drawing that forty-five. His bullet missed the sheriff no more than five inches.

Sheriff Bennett grabbed for his pistol, thinking that cowboy had shot at him and missed. A cowboy right there grabbed his hand just as it closed over the butt. "Hold it Sheriff, look behind you."

That cowboy never let go of the sheriff's hand as the sheriff looked back. A man was standing there, gun still in his hand, pointed straight down. He wobbled and dropped to his knees, releasing that pistol.

The sheriff looked back at Casey who had already holstered his forty-five. "Sorry for the scare Sheriff, Didn't have time to holler out. That ol' boy had a bead on yore back."

Sheriff Bennett said, "I damn near shot you!"

That cowboy laughed, "Naw, I saw what was happening and wasn't going to let you draw. I didn't want the kid to have to shoot you after he went an' saved yore life."

The sheriff walked back and reached down. "Chubby! What the hell? Why was you going to back shoot me?"

"One of them boys you shot with that shotgun was my cousin Ole. Couldn't let you get away with it."

"If all the dumb... Chubby I protect that town I don't give a damn if he'd been a preacher." He looked around, "Horace, you and Harvey get him over to the doctors. See if he can do anything for him."

As Chubby was carried out, the sheriff looked at Casey and smiled. "I owe you a beer cowboy. Sure wasn't expecting anything like that to happen."

"I was just about to get up and get me another beer when I saw him pull that pistol and point it at yore back. Only had time to shoot, not warn you."

The sheriff bought the beer and said, "Yeah, warning would have been too late. I's lucky you came thru our town when you did. Where are you headed?"

"Looks like Arkansas after a marshal caved my head in back at Liberty just as I was about to take two bank robbers without firing a shot."

"Bank robbers! Well I'll say. Then guess you followed them here! Are you law?"

"No Sir, not law. Yes Sir, I follered um here, but the hostler said they rode out early this morning. They'd been here two days playing poker."

That cowboy said, "Be darn! Bet yer talkin' about Louis an' Lindal lee! They's here alright. Won a good dab at the poker table."

"That's them alright. Shot my brother and ah deputy's horse over this side of Albuquerque. Maybe winning they can make it all the way to Arkansas without having to rob anybody else."

"Your brother make it?" The sheriff asked.

"Oh yeah, wadn't much just enough to keep him from comin' with me after um. It'll be my first time chasing outlaws without him, er that marshal would'a never got to clobber me. He's really good. Oh, they's four of um that robbed that bank. Got two of um in Santa Rosa, with help from the sheriff."

Casey had that beer and went to bed. In Amarillo Lindal was just about to get his butt kicked in that saloon. A fellow said with a gravelly voice, "Cowboy best you keep out'a that. They's just funnin'."

Lindal again pointed to a fellow that had a smile on his face. Red was looking everywhere for his drink. "I know I set it right there, didn't I?"

"Yeah, but I saw when he grabbed that drink an' downed it when Red wadn't lookin'."

"Last time feller, yore nose is too damn long!"

Lindal stood up, "Red I saw…"

He was hit in the right jaw driving him under that table. Sam walked over picking him up and set him in that chair.

Sam looked at Louis. "Will you tell yore friend here to keep his mouth shut when he has no idea what's goin' on."

"Oh, I think you went an' shut it for him. Lindal boy, time to stay shut an' listen for ah while."

Then all of a sudden at the bar all those cowboys started laughing and slapping Red on the back. Drinks were bought and they all yelled happy birthday, Red."

Louis smiled, "Yep, Lindal yore nose was too long but I'd say that ol' boy shortened it a bit."

"Hell, I thought I was… Yeah, wrong ah gain. Thought a damn horse kicked me."

The next morning at they rode toward Claude and Goodnight, Casey had left out of Tascosa an hour and a half before. Keeping his horse in steady lope, he knew he'd make that forty something miles before noon.

"Horse, I know this is hard on you, but it looks like plumb to Arkansas now. Best I send mama and Travis a letter lettin' um know I'm alright an' still hot on their tails." He laughed, "Yeah an' Travis will bad mouth me for not already catchin' up. Won't tell um the reason for that was ah marshal. I hope that marshal cuts his self while shavin' an' leaves ah big ol' scar."

He laughed, "Naw, maybe trip an' fall an bust his chin."

Louis and Lindal rode thru the small village of Claude and on to Goodnight before stopping.

Casey was in Amarillo eating dinner as Louis forked a piece of steak in his mouth. "Goodnight ain't nigh as big as I's thinkin' it would be. Might ought'a stayed in Claude. Bet that saloon across the road don't even got ah woman."

"I don't give ah darn if they do er not. My damn jaw still hurts where that sucker slugged me."

"Yeah, it's still ah dab swelled up alright. Finish eatin' an' we go have ah couple drinks. That'll make it feel better. Fact is it's still early, but let's take care of the horses anyhow. That way we won't have to leave ah poker game when I'm winnin."

Casey rode into Claude right at sundown and took care of his horse first thing. His head was throbbing a bit from that hot sun he had rode under today. As he started to walk up to the café, he asked the hostler,

"Think anybody in this town would have ah couple aspirin?"

"Hold on, I've got ah bottle. Be right back."

He was back in a minute and handed Casey two aspirin. "Want me to pump the water for you?"

"Naw thanks, I'll get it."

Casey took his hat off, threw the aspirin in his mouth and stuck his head under that pump. The hostler had seen his head and said, "Young feller, you wait right here." He was back in a couple minutes and handed Casey six more aspirin. "Stick them in yore pocket. Might need um when yer ah long way from ah town."

"Thanks, I'm headed for supper, you ready?"

"Naw, the wife'll have mine in ah half hour er so."

Casey ate supper and realized his headache was gone. "One beer then bed. No telling how far behind I am. Just keep trudging along until I get to Burnt Stump Road in Russellville I reckon."

If only he knew, he was only fourteen miles behind. He walked over to the saloon for a beer then went to bed. He was up and had his horse saddled, and had to wait a quarter hour for the café to open.

The cook opened the door smiling, "Come on in Cowboy. That coffee pot is ready. Kind'a early to be out, isn't it."

"Reckon, just have me ah long way to go."

"Sit, I'll get the coffee and what'll you want for breakfast?"

Thirty minutes later Casey was headed on down that road. Louis and Lindal were just eating breakfast, in no hurry. Louis said, "You know the farther east we go the hotter its gonna get. We'll shor have to keep the horses watered er they'll plumb quit on us."

"Yeah, you memmer that's why we left Arkansas to start with. Them dad gum sticky hot days an' nights, couldn't even sleep it was damn hot. Why er we even thinkin' of goin' back? We don't gotta see grandpa no how. Why not cut north up into Kansas then west into the Colorado Rockies. Yeah, that er even Wyoming. Nobody would ever think of us doin' that."

Louis looked at him and laughed, "Hell of ah idea! By dog we'll do that. Then come winter we'll ride down to Tucson then back up to the Rockies come next spring. Wish you'd thought ah that sooner."

They went for their horses and Lindal asked the hostler, "What's the closest town north of here?"

"Whoa there feller. A mighty long way. Liberal Kansas, maybe a hundred folks er so, is ah hundred miles. Then Dodge City northeast out'a there. Big cow an' railroad town Dodge City is. Still mighty rough now that the Earp's an' Doc Holladay has moved on. You won't have to look for trouble there, it'll find you in ah skipped heartbeat."

"Yeah, we've heard of it. That's where we'll head."

Louis looked at Lindal, "Gotta get grub an' coffee first. Oh an' take ah long one bottle."

Twenty minutes later they headed across country pushing hard, the thought of wild Dodge City strong on their minds. Whiskey, wild women and poker.

Louis called over, "If we'd thought ah this ah week ah go we'd already be there, maybe."

They hadn't been gone an hour when Casey rode in. "Maybe this is where they stayed the night. The hostler will darn shor know. Don't see no law office."

He stopped at the livery just as the hostler was walking in from the back lot. "Howdy young feller, Need something?"

"Yes Sir, I's wonderin' if ah couple fellers left horses here last night, one of um bein' ah right pretty red an' white paint."

"They shor nuff did. Rode out no more'n ah hour ago. Wadn't in no hurry, looked like."

"Boy howdy, I'm closer than I's thinkin. Ought'a catch um in Clarendon if they stop to eat."

"Naw, 'fraid you couldn't do that."

"Why's that? I'm on ah good horse."

"Cause they rode straight north. Headed for Dodge City's what they said."

"Naw, they's headed for Russellville Arkansas."

"Nope, stopped over at the grocery an' loaded up on grub then by the saloon for ah bottle. Saw that one stick it in his left saddle bag."

"Dodge City, can't figger why they'd change their minds about goin' to their grandpas. Any town's 'tween here an' Dodge City?"

"Not 'til you hit Liberal Kansas, over ah hundred miles, there ah bouts."

"Then I'd best get myself more supplies. And I'll take a small bag of grain along. Who knows, I might can catch um after they camp one of these nights."

"Might, but could also get ah hole blowed thru you sneakin' up on um in the dark."

"Could, hope not. I can sneak pretty good. My brother Travis showed me how when we's just kids."

CHAPTER FIVE

Louis and Lindal didn't slack up. They rode from before sunup until almost dark. Casey had no idea he was losing ground, but was following two good sets of tracks. He'd come upon a cold camp, saying, "Missed um again. They shor seem to be in ah hurry."

On the third morning around ten or so, Casey's horse threw a shoe and started limping. He dismounted and took a look. "Now why in the heck hadn't I had them checked? Horse, no tellin' how far we've gotta walk. Come to a creek it'll help."

He walked leading the horse until he couldn't walk any farther. Mounting, he let the horse take it's time and did ride up to a creek about two in the afternoon. He let the horse drink then walked him out in the water a few feet and let him stand.

"Horse, we'll stay right here for the rest of the afternoon and night. Maybe we'll make it to Liberal some time tomorrow. Neither one of them, Louis er Lindal is worth me ruinin' you. So it'll take longer. I'm young. Long's I catch um 'fore they die of old age..."

He unsaddled the horse and ate a bite then stretched out on his bedroll and napped. Louis and Lindal had arrived in Liberal an hour after noon, ate and took care of the horses. They were now in the only very small saloon with a bottle in front of them.

It took a while but before long they were playing poker with a couple local cowboys. One of them asked, "See you fellers are headed thru. Any place special er just ridin'?"

Lindal looked at his cards saying, "Thought we'd head over to Dodge City then on into Colorado."

"Huh? Dodge City shor's heck not on the way to Colorado. If it was me to save a couple hundred miles, I'd take that stage road out there up to Garden City then cut due west taking that road smack dab into Pueblo. Take ah week instead of two by not goin' all the way northeast to Dodge City. I mean less you just want to take ah chance of gettin' shot. Dodge City is still a wide-open wild town."

Louis looked over at Lindal, "What do you think?"

"I'm for Garden City. One day when we get rich, we can come back and check out Dodge City, if we want to. Course I don't want to."

One of those cowboys laughed. "Y'all plannin' on getting' rich? What er you gonna do, rob Wells Fargo?"

They all laughed at that with Louis saying, "Yeah that'd be about the only way a cowboy could get rich. That er become a politician."

That other cowboy said in a serious voice, "I shor's hell rather be called a robber than ah politician. Somebody call me ah politician I'd hurt him, bad."

The next morning Casey was mounted, walking his horse on toward Liberal. Louis and Lindal rode for Garden City.

When Casey got to town late in the afternoon, he stopped at the livery and blacksmith shop. The fellow looked up at him. "I'd say that horse lost ah shoe."

"Yes Sir, fifteen er twenty miles back. Think I could get him shod this afternoon?"

"Could I guess if I get right on it. Get him unsaddled I'll fire up them coals."

When that was done Casey said he'd go grab a bite to eat. "Say, a couple fellers might'a stopped here. One on ah red an' white paint."

"They did, headed for Garden City around seven."

"Garden City! Dang, I was told they's headed for Dodge City."

'I'd say somebody told you wrong. They headed out that stage road north."

For the next week Casey was unable to catch up. He rode thru Las Animas Colorado around two in the afternoon, knowing he could make La Junta well before dark.

He stopped at the livery and took care of his horse and three stalls down a red and white paint stuck its head out to get a look at Casey's horse. "They're here! Dog gone they're here!"

The hostler looked around, "Naw, nobody here but you an' me."

Casey walked back and saw it was the paint he was after. "When was these horses left here?"

"Last night, why?"

"Know where them fellers would be right now?"

"Yeah, same saloon they went into when they got here yesterday afternoon. The Little Brown Jug a half block up the street. Least they was still there a couple hours ah go when I walked over an' had me ah beer."

"Where's yore sheriff's office?"

"Two blocks on south. Better hurry though, he heads home to supper bout this time ever evenin'."

As Casey walked up the street, he felt his head. "Gonna see that don't happen again. I'd hate to have to shoot me ah sheriff."

He walked in the sheriff's office and a big man was just standing from his chair. "Howdy Cowboy, help you?"

"Yes Sir." Casey stuck out his hand for a shake. "Casey Pascoe from New Mexico."

The hand shake, "John Web. You've come ah long way, for something I'm thinking."

"Yes Sir. I follered bank robbers for weeks and right now I'd think they're sittin' in the Little Brown Jug. Wanted to get help if I could. Might keep me from gettin' clobbered again er shot."

"Are you law?"

"No Sir." Casey reached in his pocket giving John the papers Gus's deputy had given him.

John read those papers. "I'll say, that came over the telegraph a good while ago but it said they were thought to be headed for Arkansas."

"They was an' went over a hundred miles into Texas before for some reason they turned north up to Kansas then west to here. Should'a had um a long time 'fore now."

"Then young fellow, I'll grab another set of handcuffs and we'll go see if we can catch you a couple bank robbers."

As they walked, Casey said, "Now if they suspect anything they'll shor nuff grab iron."

"They know you?"

"Well yeah, after that Raton marshal cold cocked me down in Liberty an' let um get away, I'm shor they got a good look at me."

"Then I'd say you peek in there and let me know where they're sitting, then you go around and come in that back door. I'll give them no reason to look at me twice until I stick my forty-four in their faces. Just you wait until I get set. I'll follow your lead."

Casey said, "Best you get a beer so they'll think that's what you came after."

"That I'll do mighty close to them so I don't have to walk far. I need a beer anyhow."

They walked up and let two men walk in in front of them. Casey looking over those swinging doors spotted them right away. "Second table to our left of the back door, sittin' with three other men. They both are facing this'a way. See um?"

"Yeah, because I know them other three men. After you walk in and get set, I'll walk over and say howdy, getting their attention. That way we'll be sure we'll have no gun play."

Casey headed around the building, John walk in and a long way down the bar. The bartender smiled, "Howdy John, ready for that beer."

"Mighty nice of you to ask, Yeah I'll have one."

Casey eased in that back door and moved slowly to his right, unnoticed. He nodded his head toward the sheriff. John slowly walked over to that table while holding his beer in his left hand. "Howdy boys. Art does your wife know you're playing poker with her egg money?"

"Hell no! An' don't you go an' tell her! You'd have to jail her for murder."

"Not a word, I'll say nothing."

Acting as if he was going to turn away, he drew that forty-four just as Casey shoved his forty-five in the back of Louis's head. Lindal started his chair back but was bopped on the head with Casey's forty-five.

Louis growled, "What the hell is this..." He looked up at Casey just as Casey jerked his pistol from the holster. "You again! Sheriff this cowboy tried shooting us in the back..."

John interrupted him. "Naw, he was trying to get the drop on you like we both just did. You're both under arrest for bank robbery. Casey, get that one's pistol. He looks stupid enough to make a grab."

Casey stuck Louis's pistol in his belt then reached over taking Lindal's. "Stand, try to hit or kick it'll be yore last try. Now turn around, hands behind you."

Sheriff Web holstered his pistol and handcuffed them both. He looked down at the money that had been in front of them. "Art, how much have y'all lost, and don't lie about it, just how much?"

"I lost four dollars, same for Jeff an' Harkin."

John picked up that money and handed each man four dollars. "Enough poker for y'all get home."

He looked at Louis and Lindal, "Let's go boys, you've dragged this boy around for most to a month, wore him plumb ragged. I'd have to say he's a persistent little cuss. Don't think of but ah few lawmen could have done it."

Louis snapped, "He don't have us back to Bernalillo yet. That's ah hell of ah long ride."

Casey laughed, "Not by train it ain't so long."

"Train! You no good little son of ah…"

John slapped him up beside the head. "Be nice now, after all y'all are going on a nice train ride and will need water and food between here and there."

They were jailed and Casey said, "I need to send Sheriff Daskalas a wire telling him to send somebody after the Morgan brothers. They're in jail in Santa Rosa. I'll also wire the sheriff in Bernalillo lettin' him know I'm on the way with… Hold it! Sheriff, open that cell and search them. I'll hold a cocked pistol if they try to grab you, they won't get to go to prison."

Lindal said, "You mean they're both alive!"

"Yep, only had to shoot um a bit with the help of that sheriff. The doc said they'd be able to hang right beside you two, if that teller died."

"He ain't dead! I just shot him in the left shoulder after he tried pullin' ah gun."

"Oh, that's good. The four of you'll only get ten er twenty years."

The sheriff stuck the key in the lock when Louis said, "No need in searching us. Lindal, empty yore pockets and hand everything to the sheriff."

He unbuttoned his shirt and pulled out that bank bag, then took money from his right pocket. "That's all of it."

"Good boy, might have just saved yourself a broken jaw."

As Casey started to walk over to the depot to send those wires, John said, "I'll feed them supper, you go ahead and see about train tickets. You taking all the horses?"

"Yeah, might even keep that paint for myself."

Casey sent those wires and bought tickets for three men and three horses. Then he went and ate. He was already sitting in the saloon drinking a beer when a boy walked in with two telegrams, calling for Casey Pascoe. Casey took the telegrams and gave the boy a dime. "Thanks, Mister!"

Casey smiled as he read them. From Gus, he sent word two armed men would accompany the Morgan brothers to Bernalillo by stage. Wells Fargo would pay for those guards.

The next telegram was from Sheriff Gomez in Bernalillo. All of your prisoners will be welcomed with open arms. I have cells waiting just for those four men. Court will be swift and justice will be served.

The next morning, horses were loaded and Louis and Lindal were handcuffed to an iron bar railing that ran the length of that car.

The train pulled into Trinidad just short of noon. Casey left those two cuffed to the railing, watered the horses then got three bean burritos from a Mexican woman vender.

"Least you could'a done was brought us some coffee." Louis snarled.

Casey smiled, "Yeah, I never was a very good waiter. Forgetful, I guess. Want some water?"

The train pulled out and stopped half way up Raton Pass for coal and water. It took until late getting over Raton Pass and down into Raton. The conductor walked thru telling people there would be a delay until a steam leak behind the left driver wheels was repaired. "The hotel and café is only a half block away. Everyone will be told an' hour before we pull out. No one will be left behind."

Casey un-did those handcuffs then cuffed both their right wrist together. "We'll eat supper then I'll figger out where you two will sleep tonight. Might be handcuffed to a pole."

They ate and Louis said, "If we tell you we'll try nothin', would you take over to the saloon for one drink? You've got all our money."

Casey looked at them, "Alright we'll do that, but just so you'll know, I will not hesitate killing you both. If we have that clear, let's go."

They walked in the saloon and Casey pointed at a table. Lindal asked, "Can't you take these damn things off?"

"No! I don't want to have to shoot you. An' knowin' the liars y'all are you'd have somebody wantin' to cave my head in."

They sat, with Casey far enough away they couldn't grab him with their left hands. He called for three beers and Louis said, "I want whiskey!"

"Tough, beer or nothin'. If yer nice I might buy us two. Not nice I'll pour the first ones out an' we'll go to the livery where I'll cuff y'all to ah stall."

They downed that first beer and had just got the second one when Marshal Billingsley walked in and stopped at the bar. His whiskey was set in front of him and he slowly took a sip, while eyeballing the room.

His eyes stopped on Casey and his right hand moved down to his pistol butt. He walked toward that table. "What the hell have you gone and done cowboy? Can't quit when you're ahead."

His hand was inches away from that gun butt as Casey had seen him coming and was already standing. Casey said, "I'm doin' what I set out to do."

"Like hell you will, not in my town…" He started for his pistol but in the blink of an eye he was looking down the barrel of Casey's forty-five.

"Don't clear that holster, I don't want to kill you Marshal, but shor's hell will before I let you help these two bank robbers escape again. You helped um once. It'll not happen twice, my back ain't to you this time."

"What the hell are you taking about?"

"These two are goin' back to Bernalillo where they robbed that bank an' shot the teller. Now as soon as that train is repaired, we'll be out'a yore town. Until then you just keep the hell away from me an' my prisoners."

Louis busted out laughing. "He's ah mean little sucker, ain't he Marshal. Chased us for over a month an' even after you bashed his head in, he didn't quit an' go back home. Even said he has our two partners jailed down in Santa Rosa. I'd believe him if I's you."

The marshal stood there with his mouth open. "I, I had no idea."

"Yeah an' you shor's hell wadn't in no hurry to find out!" Casey was still mad, very mad.

"Holster your gun Cowboy, I'm sorry as can be, I was dad gum sure wrong. I'll be glad to jail them until just before train time. It'll give you some rest."

Casey looked at him. "Alright, it might give me a few hours rest an' I still have ah day and a half gettin' to Bernalillo. Fact is if you have an extra cell that's where I'll grab some shut eye."

"Let's finish our beers, while you tell me how it came about you going after um instead of law."

Just before they walked out taking Louis and Lindal to jail, the conductor walked into the saloon and shouted. "Any train passengers may as well get some sleep. It'll be sometime in the morning before the repairs are finished. I've told everyone at the hotels and cafes. I have three more saloons to visit then I'm going to bed. The train will blow the whistle a half hour before and every ten minutes until we pull out."

It was around nine the next morning, horses were fed and watered and every one climbed aboard. Louis and Lindal were re-cuffed to that rail and the train chugged forward slowly picking up speed.

Two hours later it picked up mail at Maxwell and dropped off one passenger. Then the next twenty-minute stop was Springer, then Wagon Mound and a two hour layover in Las Vegas.

Casey left those two cuffed while he fed and watered the horses then took them to eat. He asked the conductor what time they would get into Bernalillo.

"It looks like just before nine in the morning."

"Why so long, don't y'all run at night?"

"We do sometimes, but they had a flood down the west side of La Bajada and we don't want to take the chance of not seeing washed out tracks, or maybe that bridge. We'll stay in Lamy until good light. We're waiting word right now."

They got to Lamy just after midnight and the passengers were told the hotel had been notified and rooms were waiting on them. "Rooms for everyone, you'll eat breakfast at five then we roll before six if we've got no word on the track condition."

The next morning the train pulled to a stop in Bernalillo at twenty of nine. Louis and Lindal were uncuffed from that railing and cuffed together.

Then they went and unloaded the horses. Walking those blocks to the sheriff's office, Louis and Lindal walked in front. Casey walked behind leading the three horses.

A half block from the bank, the deputy sheriff had seen them coming and ran that way. The teller just started to walk into the bank and holler out, asking where the deputy was going in such a hurry.

The deputy hurried past hollering, "The bank robbers are caught and here they come."

With his left arm still in a sling, the teller drew a pistol and aimed right at Louis. The deputy stepped in the way and was shot in the lower back.

Casey saw who was shooting and at who. He grabbed his pistol as the teller hid his pistol and stepped into the bank.

The banker called out, "What was that shooting?"

The teller said, "I saw nothing."

Casey saw the downed deputy but didn't know who he was. The sheriff at hearing that shot jumped up and ran out of his office and saw Louis and Lindal, then Casey. Then he saw his deputy lying in the street. He ran up asking what the hell happened.

Louis blurted out, "This kid that's bringing us in just shot him down for no cause! Watch it Sheriff! He said he was going to kill you too!"

Both Lindal and Louis dropped to the ground as the sheriff grabbed for his pistol. Casey shot it from his hand hollering, "Sheriff! They lied I didn't shoot him I didn't even see him coming 'til he was down. The shooter ran…."

The sheriff hollered to men standing around, "You men get him! He just shot Ted! Two witnesses said so. Them are the bank robbers, don't kill them!"

Casey was wild eyed, knowing he was about to have to kill men just to stay alive. He turned, grabbed his saddle horn and hit that saddle. Turning his horse between buildings he rode out in a hurry. Every bullet fired missed everything except buildings.

The sheriff with a bloody hand picked his pistol up with his left hand and pointed it at Louis and Lindal. "At least he brought you two in. Max, hold these two while I check on Ted. Jose, run for the doctor, hurry!"

He turned Ted over and saw his eyes were closed but he was breathing. "Don't you worry Ted, I'll be on that telegraph, the bank robbers will know his name. I'll have him behind bars in no time."

Casey rode all out but saw no pursuit and slowed his horse. "Alright Casey Pascoe, you're really in for it now. Two witnesses say I shot that deputy. I go back I get jailed and maybe hung. That sheriff shor won't listen after I had to shoot that gun out of his hand. Travis I shor need yore help."

CHAPTER SIX

Casey headed for Albuquerque knowing Gus would listen. Before getting there, he turned east to the base of the Sandia Mountains. Riding on south, shirting Albuquerque by miles he talked to himself. "Nope, Gus will already have a telegram saying I shot a deputy and that sheriff. Travis, dad and mom will know how to handle this. All I have to do is not get caught an' hung before we can prove I didn't shoot that deputy."

At that very moment the doctor had just taken a slug out of that deputy's back, just below his left shoulder blade. "Another slug added to my collection. This one is mushroomed hardly at all."

Sheriff Gomez asked, "Will he make it Doc?"

"He will, be a good while recovering. He should come to within an hour or so."

"I have to get over to the depot and put it on that wire for every lawman to be on the lookout for Casey Pascoe. Why he just shot Ted down for no cause is beyond me. He brought those bank robbers in then turned his gun on Ted. I'll see he gets sent to prison for that."

"You hold on a minute! I need to look at that hand where he shot the gun out of your hand."

"Naw, its just sore where it snapped my hand side-ways. It'll be fine, but my pistol is ruined."

"You can always get a new pistol, but not a new hand. Now let me look at it then you can go send all the telegrams you want."

He sent out wires telling every lawman to be on the look out for Casey Pascoe, a deputy sheriff shooter. Then he walked back to his office and over to that cell. "How damn stupid are you two? Letting a little cowboy catch you. I'll put out a reward and hope the bounty hunters shoot him. I know that kid couldn't have shot Ted, who did?"

"Didn't see him, but it came from behind him."

"Hell I know that! He was shot in the back."

"When'll we be able to escape?"

"Not for a while, we have to make this look good. But it'll be days before your trial."

"We're gonna need money, that cowboy has ours."

****

Casey made it home just as Joel and Travis finished doing evening chores. Joel looked up with a smile, "I see you made it. I'd say those robbers are either dead or in jail."

"Jail, and that's where I'll be if I get caught."

"What in the world are you talking about?"

"I'll take care of my horse then we'll talk at supper. Mom'll want'a hear and I know she'll throw a fit, but there's nothin' I can do about that."

After the horse was taken care of, fed and watered they walked inside. All three removed their hats hanging them on the rack to the right of the door.

Tiny looked up and at seeing Casey and said, "It's about time you got yourself back. Wash up, supper is almost ready."

They all three washed their hands then sat at the table. Tiny was busy setting food on the table asking if he caught any of those men. In mid-sentence she stopped, "Good Lord! What happened to your head?"

"Just as I was about to take Louis and Lindal in Liberty, a marshal didn't like the way I had my hair parted. I'd say he did a good job."

"What happened to Lindal and Louis?"

"They got away, went into Texas then Kansas and... Mom, I have a bigger problem than almost losing them for good. Fact is if I had'a lost um I wouldn't be in all the trouble I am right now."

Tiny grabbed a chair and sat down with her mouth wide open. "What are you talking about? What kind of trouble?"

Casey told everything and Joel said, "Dad gum, sounds like you had more trouble with law than you did them four robbers."

Tiny was livid, "How blame stupid can that sheriff be, taking the word of two bank robbers against you after you brought them in?"

Casey laughed, "After shooting that gun out of his hand I wasn't gonna hang around to see how dumb he really might be. That sucker wanted all the men standing around to gun me down. I hooked um, didn't even get to hand over this bank money. Here Travis, take it to Gus. I started to go see Gus but knew he'd get a wire sayin' I'm a killer before I got there."

Travis said, "Tomorrow I'll ride in and talk with Gus. He won't believe for one dad gum minute you shot that deputy."

Joel said, "Now hold on, Casey will be wanted and if that sheriff puts out a reward, bounty hunters will sure as heck be out here looking. We'd better think this out before you let Gus know Casey is home."

Travis said, "This is the first place bounty hunters will come anyhow. Be best if Casey ain't here."

Tiny said, "I know where he'll be safe until this can all be straightened out."

"And where's that?"

"Ben Cooper's cabin on the old Ellis Ranch. No one ever goes up there except Ben."

Casey smiled, "Heck of an idea. I'll get to lay around on a stream bank and fish all day."

"I'll sack up ten days of groceries and if it's longer, Travis can bring more. It would be best you leave at daylight. No telling how long it'll take bounty hunters to get after you. I'd like to horse whip a dumb sheriff, putting my Casey in danger."

Joel said, "Now we know with witnesses even though they are lying, this is going to be tough. What do y'all think of sending for Shorty? I'd bet he would get to the bottom of this in a hurry."

Travis said, "Tomorrow when I ride in and talk to Gus, I'll send him a wire. Shor hope he ain't off somewhere on another case."

The next morning after chores, horses were saddled then they ate breakfast. Tiny handed Casey a sack of groceries and said, "I think that will last. Travis can pick us up some more beans, flour, baking soda, salt and coffee when he's in town."

They all walked out front and Casey tied that sack behind his saddle. As they mounted, Joel said, "Now

Casey, it might be best if you keep that horse in the barn out of sight. You can graze him early mornings and evenings."

"Yeah, I's thinking that. Shor hope Uncle Shorty can give a hand. If not no telling how long it'll take."

They rode out with horses in a slow lope. When they got to the bottom of Sedillo Hill, Travis said, "Careful Casey, keep that rifle handy and an eye open. I'll ride up and let you know what's goin' on ever now and ah gain."

Casey rode north taking the road toward Cerrillos and Santa Fe. Travis continued on down Tijeras Canyon toward Albuquerque.

As Travis rode past the Tijeras General Store, howdies were shouted back and forth. One boy hollered, "Hey Travis, where you go?"

"Albuquerque, want'a ride along?"

"Naw, best I don't. I have work to do, mama says."

"Might see you on the way back, Lorenzo. Don't work too hard."

"Never would I do that!"

He laughed as he heard, "Lorenzo! I need you!"

"Yes Mama, I am here."

Travis yelled back, "I'd better get before she puts me to work."

"Coward!" Was all he heard.

He rode into town and stopped at the sheriff's office. Walking in, Gus looked up. "Boy am I glad to see you! How's Casey?"

"Still has a dab of a headache now and ah gain, but hid out 'til we can clear this up. Here's that bank money, Casey at least got that."

"I'll put this on the train to the Bernalillo bank, not to that sheriff Gomez. I know all this is bull crap, but tell me Casey's side of it. I've let it go no farther than right here."

When Travis was through, Gus shook his head. "I always knew Gomez wasn't a lawman, but damned if this don't take the cake. Here Casey got all four of Gomez's bank robbers and he'd think a thing like that. What are you up to?"

"I'm sending for Uncle Shorty. He'll get to the bottom of all this, or shoot a sheriff."

"You dad gum right he will. Any bounty hunters coming in here for information will be sent towards Grant's Station and Arizona. I'm sure you boys know how to keep Casey hid out."

"Oh yeah, no problem there. Just hope Uncle Shorty ain't off somewhere."

"Me too, he'll most likely stop off here before riding out to y'all's place. I'll tell him everything I know and how that little Casey got everyone of those robbers by his self."

Travis stood, "Best I get that telegram sent. The sooner Uncle Shorty gets it the sooner he'll get here."

He rode back down to the depot and this is the wire that was sent: U.S. Marshal Shorty Thompson. B&S Ranch old Fort Tularosa, Catron County New Mexico. 'Uncle Shorty, Casey is in trouble… Needs your help in a hurry.'

"Well Travis, that'll get to Socorro in a few minutes and be on the morning stage west. Four days from now he'll be here or he won't."

"Thanks Jessup, if I'm back in town I'll drop by just to see if he answers when he gets to Socorro."

"I'd doubt that. He'll just put Dunnie on the train and come on."

"Yeah, reckon yer right. If dad didn't need help with the chores, I'd just stay in town an' wait on him."

"Uh huh, and be bored out'a your mind. Go on home Travis and be useful." He smiled as did Travis.

"Yer right, late as it is I'll stay tonight and have a couple beers at the Liberty and talk with Chris and Millie."

"Yeah, meant to ask, why in the world are you favoring that left arm?"

"Got shot just over a month ago no more than three miles from the house."

"The hell you say!"

"Yeah, by the same bank robbers Casey went ah head an' got. That's why we need Shorty's help. Seems as some law ain't nothin' but idiots. Least Casey shor ran into two of um that shor nuff is."

"Travis, I don't want you getting mad at me, but I need to ask you a question."

"Naw, questions don't make me mad if my answers don't make you mad." He smiled.

"Dog gone it I know you went all the way thru school. Didn't your teacher teach you proper English?"

"Oh, you mean like enough, sure thing and going to and wasn't and you are...? Well yeah, but who in the hell would understand me?"

The depot man looked at him then smiled, "Shor nuff Travis, got-cha. Know zackly what you mean."

Travis turned to walk out, "Have a nice afternoon, Mister Kindal. I'm going to and will share it with you."

"I'll even buy you a beer if you're still at the Liberty when I get off work." Mister Kindal shook his head.

"Pulling my leg is what that boy was doing."

****

Casey rode up to Ben's cabin before middle afternoon. He rode over to the barn and by dog, Ben's horse was in the first stall.

He tied his horse and walked over to the house knocking on the door, no answer. "Well shoot, wonder where he got off to?'

He walked back to the barn, stopped and said, "The creek!"

He walked down to the creek and sure enough there was Ben hauling in a trout. Ben smiled, "Saw you when you rode in but didn't want to holler out. I had that trout nibbling on my line for over a half hour. Howdy Casey, good to see you. What are you doing over this'a way."

"Came to see if I could stay awhile."

"You most certainly can! Be glad for the company."

He picked up a string of fish saying, "I guess you'll help me eat these for supper."

"Shor's heck will. What er you doin' over here in the middle of the week."

"Boss fired me so I'm takin' time off to get my fishin' in."

"Fired you, for what?"

"Drunk on the job. Course I wadn't, I had a bad cold and the doc gave me some foul tastin' stuff that smelled like whiskey er wine. He smelled it on me an' fired me on the spot. I thanked him an' rode up here three days ago."

They walked up to the house and Ben said, "You go ah head and take care of yore horses while I clean these fish."

"Yeah, and mama sent a whole sack full of food."

"Hope there's coffee. I only have enough for maybe a couple more days."

"Knowin' mama, she shoved in a whole sack."

An hour later they were sitting on the porch eating fish and drinking beer. Ben asked why Casey was staying awhile.

When told Ben got mad. "Maybe I ought'a just ride down to Bernalillo and do away with a stupid sheriff."

"Naw, words out I shot the deputy and I did shoot the gun out of the sheriff's hand. He shows up dead folks would just know I'm the one that went an' done it. I shor can't believe that sucker after I brought them two robbers in a' two more on the way."

"Yeah, guess yer right. Think y'all's uncle Shorty'll be able to help?"

"I'd think so, don't see why not. One thing he'd know for shor is I'd never shoot no deputy 'less he was shootin' at me first. Ben, it took me over a month to get them last two. Wish now I hadn't done it an' just gone on back home after that marshal parted my hair. I'd shor be better off an' not wanted by the law."

"Any idea who did shoot that deputy?"

"I saw him good. Had his left arm in a sling. Couldn't do nothin' holdin' on to them bank robbers. Then that dumb sheriff came runnin' up an' things really went to hell in ah hurry."

As they sat and talked, Sheriff Gomez had stopped by the doctor's office to check on Ted while on his way home to supper.

Ted sat up saying, "Sheriff, the doc told me the boy that brought in Louis and Lindal shot me. It couldn't have been him. I was shot in the…"

"Now just stop worrying about it. I have two witnesses that saw the whole thing. If the law can't get him, bounty hunters sure will. You just get better and you'll be back to work in no time."

"Yes, but Sheriff…"

"I have to get on to the cafe, supper is waiting. The doctor said you'd be able to go home in a few days."

"Yes, but Sheriff..." Again, he was shut down and the sheriff walked out.

Ted was mad. "Doctor, I never realized just how hard headed the sheriff is. He gets something in his head there's no changing it. That boy did not shoot me, he couldn't have."

"How can you say that?"

"I was walking straight toward him when I was shot in the back."

"You mean you didn't turn to look back at Sheriff Gomez. I was told that's what happened."

"I don't care what you were told, those men lied and the sheriff believed them."

"Then I hope that boy is brought in alive where he can tell his side of it."

"I think the sheriff is just mad he got his pistol shot out of his hand with over a dozen people watching."

The doctor laughed, "Now that could be. Proved he's not as fast as he once might have been. Oh, here's your folks to take you home."

"You mean I can go home now, tonight!"

"Yes, bedrest only. Don't you be up and around until I tell you, you can be."

In the Liberty Saloon in Albuquerque, Travis was having a beer with friends when two bounty hunters walked in. One bellowed out, "We're lookin' for ah Casey Pascoe! Anybody here know him?"

Men shook their heads no, but Travis said, "Yeah, I know him. Rode with him ah few years."

They both walked over to Travis's table as other men wonder what the hell Travis was up to. "What does he look like?"

"You mean yer after a feller an' don't even know what he looks like?"

"Well yeah, no description on this poster. Just says a two hundred dollar reward for Casey Pascoe."

Travis stood, "Two hundred dollars! You mean I grab him I get two hundred dollars!"

"Back off cowboy, he's ours, now what does he look like?"

"Well yeah, I wouldn't go up against him no how. He's gooder than me with ah gun, rifle er pistol. He's around forty with a big black handle-bar mustache. Has a scar runnin' down his left cheek. Limps with his left leg where he took ah bullet years back. Two days ago, when I saw him last, he was headed west torge Grant's Station. Then maybe Arizona. Seemed to be in one heck of ah hurry."

"He's got reason, he shot ah deputy in Bernalillo."

"Naw, Casey! Darn, that son of ah gun. Was it over a beer?"

"What?"

"Was it over a beer? Casey gets testy when anybody messes with his beer."

"What the hell difference does it make what it was over? Nobody shoots ah deputy an' gets away with it, not when bounty hunters gets after him."

"Now I shor do need two hundred but wouldn't try Casey just to get it."

"That's our job we'll get him. How far's this Grant's Station?"

"Seventy miles er so. He'd be there by now."

"We'll ride out come mornin'. Come on Sonny, let's go eat a bite."

After they left, that whole saloon roared in laughter. "Shame on you Travis, telling on your own brother that'a way."

That brought more laughter.

CHAPTER SEVEN

Three days later U.S. Marshal Shorty Thompson unloaded his dun stud from the train in Albuquerque. Leading him down to the livery he took care of him then walked the several blocks up to the sheriff's office. "Howdy Gus."

"Shorty, glad you made it, for Casey's sake. Sit, I'll tell you all I know. I did hear bounty hunters are already on it, but Travis sent the first two toward Arizona. It'll be a while before they're back."

"Boy howdy I knew there was real trouble when I got that wire from Travis. Do you know anything about that sheriff Gomez? I mean other than him being a total idiot."

"Not much, heard stories is all. Most not that good, can't be much of a law man thinking Casey would shoot that deputy after bringing in those bank robbers."

Shorty stood, "I've already taken care of Dunnie. Best I get something to eat then have a beer er two. I'll ride out to Pascoe's tomorrow and talk with them. Hope

Casey knows how to stay hid out for no tellin' how long. Oh, what did you say happened to them last two robbers?"

"They were taken on over to Bernalillo. I have no idea if they've gone to trial or not. Gomez says Louis and Lindal Lee are his witnesses against Casey. So, I'd think he still has them in jail until Casey is caught. Oh, Travis even brought me that bank money Casey took off those men."

"Yep, them are good boys. Care for a beer 'fore you head home to supper?"

"May's well, Chris and Milly will be glad to know you came to help Casey."

"Bein' his uncle I'd done it even if I wadn't ah marshal. Them boys was brought up right."

The next morning Shorty rode out to the Pascoe's and Travis saw him riding in, "Dad, here comes Uncle Shorty. Now things will start to happen."

Joel walked from the barn just as Shorty rode up. "Howdy, Shorty, step down. Got coffee on the stove."

"Then let's have ah cup an' talk."

He stepped from the saddle dropping the reins. Dunnie walked over to the water trough as the three of them walked into the house.

Tiny with a big smile said, "I guess trouble is all it took for you to come visiting. Hello Shorty, sit and I'll get the coffee."

"Well sis, I've been kept pretty busy, except when I'm fishing." He laughed and pulled out a chair.

As coffee was set in front of them, Shorty asked, "Where my little buddy, Casey?"

"He's staying up at Ben Cooper's cabin."

"Heck of an idea. He'll darn shor not be seen up there. I'll ride by and spend the night with him on my way to Bernalillo. I'm going to have me a long talk with a stupid sheriff."

They sat around and talked while Tiny fixed dinner. Then they ate and Shorty said, he'd best ride and make Ben's before dark.

Tiny said, "Travis needs to ride up there anyhow and take more coffee, beans and potatoes."

"Be glad for the company. Travis, get saddled up."

Twenty minutes later they rode out and did make Ben's before sundown though the sun had been behind the mountains for over an hour.

Ben and Casey were just thru feeding the horses when they rode up. "Uncle Shorty, shor am glad you made it. Travis, I guess mom sent coffee."

"She did."

Shorty said, "Howdy Ben, Casey. Let's get these horses taken care of. Which one of y'all is the cook?"

Ben laughed, "I am! Casey even burns water. You ever try any of his coffee?"

"Naw, lucky I guess."

"Now come on you guys! I hadn't killed myself yet eatin' my own cookin'."

Shorty smiled saying, "Yeah but yer still young."

They laughed, talked and enjoyed each other's company. Ben did cook a good supper, pinto beans, deer steak and biscuits, four inches round.

As they ate Shorty asked Ben how he learned to cook so darn good. "My little sis, took her forever but she sure was patient."

After supper Casey helped Ben with the dishes and Travis asked Shorty, "Do you want any of us to ride down to Bernalillo with you?"

"Naw, best not. Not right off anyhow. I need to pull this badge off an' do some nosin' around. Might talk with the doctor an' see what kind'a slug was took out'a that deputy. It'd help if he's alive. But that slug will let me know what caliber. That could tell the whole story…

Wait, you said the feller that did shoot him had his left arm in a sling. Can't be too many fellers in Bernalillo with a bad left arm."

Casey said, "I shor didn't hang around to find out if that deputy was dead er not. Heck, I didn't even have time to take that money over to the bank. Travis took it into Gus."

"Yeah, he told me. One day when this is settled, I'll see Wells Fargo gives you that reward. That er I'll rob a Wells Fargo bank and give you the money."

They all laughed at that.

Shorty rode out after breakfast and stopped at Placitas and ate dinner. He had his badge in his pocket and felt good no one knew he is a marshal.

Slow riding on down to Bernalillo took under three hours and he stopped and watered Dunnie at the town horse trough. Looking around he saw the doctor's office and knew that's where he go after he had himself a beer and ask a few innocent questions about a deputy sheriff being shot.

Also, he'd get a feeling of what folks thought of their sheriff. Though it was just after middle of the afternoon, several horses were tied in front of that first saloon. Before dismounting, he looked around but didn't see the sheriff's office.

He tied Dunnie and walked in and stood at the bar, waiting for a beer. The bartender walked over and wiped the bar in front of him asking what he wanted to drink. "Beer."

No one paid him any mind so the moved over to a table with his back to a wall. He listened while drinking that beer, but nothing was said of the shot deputy. He got up and took his mug to the bar and as he set it down, he said, "Say, bartender, heard y'all got yore deputy sheriff shot a while back. Did he make it?"

"Yeah, his father was in night before last and said he is coming along just fine."

"Boy howdy that's good to hear. They catch who it was that shot him."

"No, he rode off like the coward he is. Shooting Ted in the back the way he did."

"Oh, you mean the skunk snuck up behind him an' shot him?"

"No I... He... By jacks I never heard how it came about. Sheriff Gomez put a two-hundred-dollar reward on him. He'll be caught anytime now."

"Then he was seen an' everybody knows who he is."

"Yeah, brought in two bank robbers then just turned his gun on Ted for no reason."

"Now that's pretty cold hearted to bring in robbers then shoot the deputy. Can't figger out why he'd do somethin' like that. Did he collect the reward for them robbers?"

"Naw, rode off without it after the sheriff ran up to arrest him. Shot the sheriff's gun out of his hand."

"By dog, looks like if he just shot that deputy, he'd shot the sheriff dead center."

The bartender looked at him, "Yeah, huh, wonder why he didn't."

"Maybe he didn't shoot the deputy."

"Oh yeah, two witnesses saw him do it. Told the sheriff too. And his name was Casey Pascoe."

"You don't say! This deputy Ted, does he live close by?"

"Three blocks west toward the river."

"Well long's he'll pull thru that's the main thing. I've gotta take care of my horse. Most likely be back after a bit."

He walked out and got Dunnie and rode back down to the doctor's office. Walking in, the doctor looked up. "How can I help you, cowboy?"

"Doc, came to talk about that deputy that was shot."

"What about him?"

"Heard he was shot in the back, but the boy that was supposed to have done it was walking toward him. How is that possible?"

"It isn't. Even Ted is very sure it wasn't him. He can't figure out why Sheriff Gomez keeps insisting it was that boy that brought in the robbers."

"Well for sure I know he didn't do it. Do you have that slug?"

"Right here." He reached behind him and picked up that slug, handing it to Shorty.

Shorty smiled, "Hang on to this, it proves Casey wasn't the shooter."

"How's that?"

"Casey uses a forty-five, not a forty-four."

"Are you sure? How in the world would you know that?"

"Because Casey Pascoe is my nephew and I know him darn well…"

"You are that young man's uncle!"

"I am and am also a U.S. Marshal. As I said Doc, hold on to that and keep our conversation to yore self. If this thing goes to court it'll prove wrong bullet, wrong man. Tell no one I'm looking into this, I don't want'a get back shot. Oh, the shooter was wearing a sling on his left arm. You bein' the only doc, how many fellers around here are using a sling."

"Only one, that's the bank teller. He was the one the robbers shot."

"Then I'd say he was trying to get even and shot the wrong man. When he saw what he'd done he panicked and ran."

The doctor looked at him. "Now that is very possible. It happened about the time Clinton would be getting to the bank, and very close. How can you be sure and maybe make him tell the truth."

"Break his other arm." Shorty laughed, "Naw I'll threaten the hell out of him. I'll tell him I'll put him on the stand and if he lies, he'll get five years. I'll do all of that later, first off, I need to find out why the sheriff took the word of two bank robbers over the man's word that brought them in. Now I need to talk with Ted, where could I find him?"

"Home, take that next street. They live three blocks on the right. It's the only house with a fenced yard. They have a dog."

Shorty said thanks and started to walk out. The doctor asked, "Do you know if that boy Casey is safe?"

"He is and has darn good help if bounty hunters show up."

Shorty walked out to Dunnie and rode those three blocks. Dismounting, he dropped the reins and opened that gate as a barking dog came running around the house.

Shorty held out his hand saying, "Hold it boy and neither of us will get hurt."

Mrs. Hubble heard the dog barking and came to the door. Calling dog she asked, "Can I be of help?"

"Yes Ma'am, I'd shor like to talk with Ted. The doctor told me where y'all live."

"Just a moment, I'll get him." She walked back inside and Shorty eased on up close to the porch so they talk and wouldn't have to holler to be heard.

Ted and his mother walked out, she wanted to make sure he wasn't going to hurt her son.

"Ted, I'm Shorty Thompson Casey Pascoe's uncle."

"You are! Come on up and sit down. Boy howdy do I have a lot to tell you, you or anyone else that would listen. Sheriff Gomez sure won't."

Shorty walked up on the porch and they sat down. Ted asked, "First off, do you know if Casey is alright? Sheriff Gomez is hoping bounty hunters will bring him in or kill him."

"Casey is mighty fine, not a worry in the world. Bounty hunters will get nowhere close to him. Now you have no idea who shot you?"

"No, but by darn sure know it wasn't Casey. He was walking those two robbers toward me. The only one I saw behind me was... Naw, Clinton wouldn't have shot me!"

"Yep, 'fraid he did. Casey said the shooter was wearin' his left arm in a sling. The doc said that teller is the only feller in town wearin' one."

"I'll be darn, why would he do that?"

"I'd say he was takin' ah shot at the fellers that shot him an' got you by mistake."

"Now that sure could be right. I heard him say he'd like to get them in his gun sights."

"Now partner, don't you er yore folks breathe a word of this. I still have some lookin' in to do an' don't want'a get back shot doin' it."

"Oh no, not a word as you're trying to help Casey. I'm sure glad you're here. I feel a lot better now. I was so worried about him and there was nothing I could do. What will happen to Clinton?"

"That I don't know. We do know he didn't shoot you on purpose. He's just scared, I'm shor."

"Yeah, he came to see me a lot when I was at the doctor's, just checking on me."

Shorty stood, "I'll be around for a few days until I can get to the bottom of a few things. I'm shor you'll hear how it comes out. I may have to bring Casey in here for trial. I do I'll shor need you to testify. One thing, I do have solid proof Casey didn't shoot you. Wrong bullet, wrong man."

"I'll sure be glad to hear what it is. Dad gum it he risk his life to bring those robbers in, now look at the trouble he's in."

"That's what you call a dumb sheriff. I'll get it straightened out, might take ah while."

"Good luck. You need me for anything, I'll be right here."

Shorty left with a smile on his face. He could go to the judge right now and clear Casey, but he wanted to find out more about why Gomez took the word of two robbers.

Mrs. Hubble also had a smile on her face. "Ted, I think you can now stop worrying about Casey Pascoe. That young man seems to be a tough go getter. He'll get to the bottom of this."

Shorty headed to the livery and took care of Dunnie, then ate supper and went to that saloon for a beer or two. He just might get to see Sheriff Gomez.

CHAPTER EIGHT

As Shorty sat in that saloon drinking beer, Sheriff Gomez was standing in front of that cell getting cussed out. Louis said, "I don't give a damn if that kids' ever caught. By damn we've been in here long enough. Get us some horses and bring them around back and we'll get the hell out of here. We'll head up to Durango an' maybe Cortez. We won't ever be back here so don't worry."

"How in the hell am I going to get four horses without questions being ask?"

"That hostler has gone home by now, get um! Hell, let us out an' we'll get um."

"No! We'll have to make this look good so they won't know I had anything to do with letting you out."

He stood there a moment longer. "Alright, it'll take me a half hour to get the horses and bring them up the back alley."

Forty-five minutes later he walked in that back door. Getting the key to the cell he was talking. "Alright, I brought this rope." He Opened the cell. "Now tie me up and gag me on that bunk. Now damn it don't be seen or lead will fly. Oh, your guns are in that lower drawer. And lock this cell and just drop the key on the floor out of reach."

Charlie and Reese had to have help with their gun belts, but ten minutes later they were ready to go. "We need money."

"I don't have any money here! Just gag me and ride before someone comes in."

He was tied and gagged, the cell was locked and the key dropped in the middle of the floor. Out that back door they went, grabbing horses. Reese and Charlie had to be handed the reins as Lindal asked, "What in the hell are we going to do without money?"

Louis smiled, "By damn we'll have money, come on." They rode on up the alley and stopped behind the bank. "Charlie, you and Reese get them guns out'a them holsters an' wait right here. Come on Lindal, we're gonna rob us ah bank."

They walked over and Louis, with two hard kicks busted that back door open. Lindal asked, "How'n the hell are we gonna get in that safe?"

"It's open, remember when we robbed it the banker didn't have to use that combination. That lock is broke, 'less he got it fixed."

Louis turned that handle and smiled as that door was swung wide. He grabbed a sack and shoved all the paper money in it. Lindal asked, "What about all them gold an' silver coins?"

"Grab another bag, get what you can, we have to get the hell out of here. I want to be miles gone before we stop for the night. Gomez will have to get up a posse after he's found just to make it look good."

They walked out that back door, leaving it open. Louis laughed as he told Charlie and Reese, he got a whole bag of money. "Even Gomez will be surprised when he hears the bank was robbed."

They kept to the back streets headed west, northwest toward Aztec and Durango. "Well boys we got a lot more money this time and didn't have to half it with Gomez. That'll make a jaw twitch when he finds out how much we got. No matter, we ain't ever comin' back here no way."

Charlie said, "Least that damn kid won't be on our tails. He's worse that ah damn blood hound."

Lindal laughed, "Yeah, I think me an' Louis prodly already went an' got him shot by now. Shor fooled ol' Gomez. Me an' Louis both saw who shot that deputy. It was that damn teller we went an' shot. Bet he was tryin' for one of us. Glad he's ah lousy shot."

They rode about fifteen miles and camped right beside the road. They knew they had to make Jemez Springs just to get a bite to eat. They'd also buy trail grub and plenty of coffee. Louis knew there was nothing but stage stops for over a hundred and fifty miles. Aztec would be the first saloon and they not only had no food they had no whiskey.

****

Shorty sat in that saloon longer than he wanted to, but darn it he wanted to get a look at Sheriff Gomez. "One more beer, then I'm headed for bed."

He walked over to the bar and asked for a refill and asked, "Don't y'all's sheriff go into saloons?"

"Yeah, must have already gone home. Didn't even stop by for his normal glass of whiskey."

"Heard he was a mighty tough sheriff."

The bartender looked at him. "Ever who told you that is out of his damn head! He ain't law, he's a damn mooch. Never pays for anything. If it wasn't for that little deputy Ted, we'd have no law. Now he's laid up for no tellin' how long. Went an' got shot by the same little cowboy that brought in them bank robbers."

"Nope yer wrong on that."

"What do you mean?"

"How can anybody shoot somebody in the back while walking straight toward one another? Can't be done, don't make ah damn what that sheriff said."

The bartender looked at him. "By damn yer right! Why didn't Gomez think of that?"

"Maybe he didn't want to. I think folks needs to vote him out'a office."

"Nobody'll run against him, 'fraid to."

"Then the sucker is tough, that what yer sayin'?"

"No that's not what I'm saying! The last two men that ran against him was shot dead while Gomez stood in here drinking my whiskey. They were just found shot dead."

"Yep, I'd be afraid to run against him myself. I'll just go on to bed and meet him another time."

The next morning Shorty sat eating breakfast, listening to other customers talk. One said, "Haven't seen our sheriff strutting around this morning. He'll be in after a bit for his free coffee and breakfast."

Other men laughed and started talking about other things. Shorty finished his meal and went down to the livery to check on Dunnie and give him a rub down.

As he brushed and combed Dunnie the hostler said, "Least they didn't take yore dun an' he's the best lookin' horse in here."

"Somebody take ah horse?"

"Yeah, four of um saddles an' all. Meanin' they was rode and not lead with ah rope around their necks."

"Could it ah been the owners, er was they yours?"

"Naw, the owners of two of um's in jail. The other two belonged to a couple cowboys from the Quail Ranch. I loaned um ah couple just to get home on. They'll bring um back in ah couple days."

"Stupid is all I can say. Horse thieves are hung if caught, without a trial."

Shorty finished Dunnie and put him back in the stall. "Being as I ain't doin' nothin' I think I'll go have one more cup of coffee then maybe walk up and meet y'all's sheriff."

"Why in the hell would you want'a do that? You want to talk with somebody with ah brain, talk to yore horse." He laughed saying, "When you meet him, you'll see what I mean. That's one thick headed sucker. For somebody that knows nothin', he knows it all. He'll argue about day er night."

Shorty walked back to the café for that cup of coffee and talk a bit. Maybe he ought to look up the judge and have a talk with him. After all, with that .44 slug he had solid proof. Ted could tell that Casey could not have shot him. First thing he needed to get those bounty hunters called off before some of them got themselves shot.

"Hold it! Shoot fire, I'll take Clinton by the nap of his neck and let him tell the judge!" He looked around embarrassed as everyone in there was looking at him.

"Sorry folks, got carried away." He dropped a dime on that table and walked out.

Checking his watch, the bank wouldn't open for another ten minutes. He looked at the bank just as the banker and teller walked up, opening the front door.

Shorty smiled, "I'll let um get…"

Out that bank door ran the banker screaming the bank had been robbed. Shorty headed that way but the banker was on his way to the sheriff's office.

Shorty said, "Time to talk with Clinton while nobody is around."

He walked in the bank and Clinton said, "I'm sorry Mister, the bank was robbed and we are closed."

"Yeah, heard the banker as he was runnin' down the street. Clinton, do you have any idea how much danger you put that feller in that brought in those bank robbers? Bounty hunter are after him."

"What? I don't know what you mean!"

"Yeah you do, being as you was the one that shot the deputy." Shorty reached over and jerked that forty-four out of his waist band. "I can prove that slug came from this gun, yore gun."

The teller was sacred plumb white. "It was an accident! I didn't mean..."

They heard the banker running back down the street screaming his head off. "The sheriff's been robbed! No! No! The banks been robbed and the sheriff is locked in his own cell."

Out that door Shorty went, passing men as they all headed for the sheriff's office. Two men were standing in front of that cell looking at the sheriff tied and gagged on that bunk.

Shorty saw the key on the floor and picked it up. Walking over he opened the cell and untied the sheriff. "What the hell happened? I see all four of your prisoners are gone."

"Like an idiot, alone I was going to let two at a time go to the outhouse. They jumped me and tied me up. Get out of my way! I have to get up a posse!"

Shorty said, "Yeah and before they left town, they robbed the bank, again."

"What? Good Lord no!"

Shorty asked, "What time last night did this happen?"

"I don't know, just after eight, I guess. I was just getting ready to go to the saloon for my whiskey when they called out needing to use the outhouse."

"Don't even think of a posse, they have over a twelve hour head start. I'll get my own help and go after them myself."

"You! Just who in the hell do you think you are?"

"U. S. Marshal Shorty Thompson. And before I go, you get on that telegraph and call off that warrant you have out on Casey Pascoe."

"Why in the hell would I do that?"

"Because the bank teller is who shot yore deputy in the back, not Casey. Wrong bullet, wrong man."

"How in the hell do you know that?"

"A forty-four slug was what the doctor took out of the deputy. Casey uses a forty-five and couldn't have shot him in the back walking toward him."

"Now you look here… How do you know what caliber gun he uses?"

"Partner, I'm the one that taught him how to shoot and bought him that forty-five when he was fourteen years old. You see, he's one of my favorite nephews. So, if anything at all happens to Casey, you'll go to prison or I'll shoot you dead! Now get the hell over to that depot and do yore damn job! Any of these men here can go to the bank and talk with Clinton. He'll talk now, I scared the hell out of him."

Gomez hot footed it toward the depot and one of the men asked Shorty, "Marshal, that Casey, is he alright?"

"He is and I'll have him back here with me by tomorrow night. We have four escaped bank robbers to go after."

"But that will give them an almost a three day's head start. Think you can catch them?"

"Without a doubt, they'll stop at saloons and get drunk on bank money and play poker. All I have to do is find out which way they rode out. Not south, not east, so that leaves north or west. I'm bettin' west because no telegraphs."

"Damn, you're sure smarter than Gomez!"

"Well now that's something. I'm going for my horse and I'll be back tomorrow evening late."

He rode out pushing hard as Gomez sent telegrams calling off bounty hunters. He stepped from the depot, scared to his toes. "A damn U.S. Marshal! I have to calm down, he has no way of tying any of this to me. I'll just go on about my… Wait! He said he was going after them! What if he does catch them? I've got to get to them first! I know where they are going, he doesn't!" He headed for the livery.

"Henry, saddle my horse. I'll be riding in ten minutes."

"Where are you headed?"

"After those prisoners, they escaped and robbed the bank again."

"Yeah, I heard. You messed up ah again, huh?"

"Drop it Henry! Get my horse!"

Ten minutes later he went back to his office and got his rifle and two boxes of cartridges. Opening his desk, he opened a box and took out his huge stash of money. Sticking that in a money belt, he strapped it around his waist. "Trail supplies! I can't forget those and two canteens. Darn, I'll need my bedroll and it's at the house. Calm down, calm down you have at least a two day's head start on that marshal and less than a day behind Louis and them. Wonder who he's going after for help. He said two days. I sure hope it isn't a good tracker."

He laughed, "That won't matter as much of a head start as we'll have. He'll never catch us. And there's no way he'll know which way we've headed."

He let folks know he was going after those robbers. "Ted will be up before long he can handle things. It's my job, I'll catch them or won't be back!" He rode out, horse in a lope, laughing his butt off. "Hell no, I'm not coming back."

****

Shorty made it to Ben's just at sundown and unsaddled Dunnie. Casey and Ben got feed while they were talking.

"Well Casey, you was right, it was the teller that shot the deputy. That Gomez is as big of an idiot as I've ever seen. Those robbers you brought in broke out last night and re-robbed the bank. We're goin' after um."

As they walked to the house Ben asked, "What do you think of me riding along?"

"If you want to, no telling how long we'll be. They'll have better than a two days head start."

"Yeah, I want'a go. Beats the hell out of sittin' around here talkin' to myself. Least I'll have company. Matter of fact we can take part of my grub so packrats don't get it. Casey, let's get supper. Oh, Shorty, I'm plumb out'a beer. We drank it all waitin' on you."

Shorty laughed, "I can do without until we get back to Bernalillo tomorrow evening. Casey, don't you smart off at that sheriff. He was tied and gagged in his own cell. Yeah, upset somewhat."

"That gag should help. At least his mouth was shut where he could hear something. Boy howdy he wouldn't listen to nothin' I was tryin' to say. Then like a dummy and me holdin' my gun, he tried goin' for his. Way things turned out I should'a put ah slug in him. Then they'd really had a reason to chase me."

They ate supper laughed and talked until bed time. Morning came and Shorty awoke to the strong smell of coffee. He walked in and sat at the table asking, "Ben, don't you ever sleep?"

"Once in a while. Just excited about gettin' the heck away from here for no telling how long."

Shorty said, "Lead might fly our way."

"Might, I'll worry about that the same time you do. I'm using the last bit of my flour and makin' flapjacks this morning. Didn't want it to go stale."

Casey and Travis came walking in asking, "What the heck time is it? Don't y'all sleep?"

Shorty said, "It'll be day light out there soon. We want'a be ridin' as soon as it is."

Travis said, "When we get to Bernalillo, I need to send a telegram to Gus lettin' him know what we're doin' an' he can send somebody out an' let mom and dad know we won't be back for some time."

Casey said, "Yeah, no need in um worrin' about you too. I keep gettin' into trouble it'll give mama gray hair. Then she'll really be upset. Yep. I can hear her now, Casey Pascoe, this is all your fault! Around mom there's no chance I'd ever forget my name."

They laughed and ate breakfast. While Ben and Travis did dishes and cleaned and put everything away, Shorty and Casey saddled all the horses. They rode out a half hour later.

Making it to Placitas well before noon, they didn't stop, just rode on that seven or so miles downhill into Bernalillo. They watered the horses then tied up in front of a café.

As they ate, they talked. Shorty said, "I know it's just after noon, but if we rode out now, we wouldn't get no more'n twenty miles. We leave out early in the morning we can make the first stage stop by night."

Ben said, "Then while you do what you have to, maybe me an' Travis can have us a beer, er two."

"We'll all go have a beer, that's where I'll find out a few things. Then I'll leave y'all and go talk to the judge an' see what he wants to do with Clinton."

They walked into an almost empty saloon and sat at a table. The bartender walked over smiling, "Well Cowboy, you shor do got folks talkin' you bein' ah U.S Marshal. They think somethin' will get done now. Them robbin' the bank again shor hurts folks until Wells Fargo gets here an' makes it all good."

"Yeah, we'll get after um come mornin' Might take ah while but we'll bring all that money back they ain't spent. We push hard they'll be too busy runnin' to spend much."

"Yeah, and Gomez has already gone after um."

"He what! How'd he know which way they went?"

"Hell, I don't know, he rode out yesterday around noon. Said it was his job to get um."

"He'll mess around an' get his self shot. I may be wrong but I'd say he couldn't find his left hand if it wadn't growed on."

By late afternoon the saloon started filling up and Shorty said he'd go find that judge. "After I do that, we'll go over an' eat supper."

Shorty walked out and not five minutes later, several fellows walked in and got drinks. As they looked around, one saw Ben and walked over.

"Howdy Ben, hadn't seen you in ah while."

"Nope, hadn't been over this'a way in months."

"What about my sister?"

"What about her?"

"Ain't y'all gonna marry up?"

"Hell no! What ever gave you that idea?"

"Her, said you danced with her at that street dance six weeks ah go."

"Danced with four different girls that night an' I ain't gonna marry any of um."

"Think yer too good for my sister, that it?"

"Drop it Max, I just ain't gonna get married."

"Did you ever hear of ah shotgun wedding?"

"Did you ever hear of gettin' yore nose busted!"

"Go to hell Ben Cooper!" He stomped off.

Casey laughed, "Thought you'd jump at the chance to marry up."

"You thought wrong! You ought'a see his sister. She's bigger an' uglier than he is."

CHAPTER NINE

Gomez had traveled that stage road until after sundown, then slowed his horse to a walk. He was looking for a place to camp before dark with no moonlight to see by.

He pulled off to the side of the road and sat down, looking up at his horse. He got up and tied the bridle reins to a dead stomp and reached up getting his sleep blanket and small pillow.

Rolling it out he laid down, now even thinking of removing that saddle. A few hours later a wolf howled waking him. "Damn, that's close."

He rolled up his sleeping blanket and tied it behind the saddle. Then untied his horse and mounted. The moon was over head and very bright. He kicked that horse out to a long lope wondering if he would catch those men in Aztec, or would it be Durango.

Louis and Lindal, Charlie and Reese were snoring away. Thirty miles in front of him. That was a day and a half ago, now they were in Aztec half drunk and Gomez was coming on strong.

What he didn't know, Shorty and three men had talked to the stage driver and he told where he met four riders then the next day met Gomez. Shorty said, "Don't seem to be making such good time."

They were now also picking up ground. They were less than two days back and knew they were on the right trail but it could be as long as maybe a week before they caught up.

Around ten that morning Gomez rode up to the stage stop and trading post called Blanco. He watered his horse and smelled that food.

Taking his time, he ate a very large meal and asked when four riders stopped here. "They stayed the night and rode out a couple hours after sunup. Even before eating supper, they drank a whole bottle of whiskey and took two bottles with them."

"Then that means they would have left Aztec this morning."

"I'd say so and over half way to Durango by now. They'll make that shortly after noon."

"Then I should make it to Durango by tomorrow night. Don't you think?"

"Shouldn't be no problem if you keep moving. You could even make Aztec this afternoon, maybe an hour er so after sundown. Then a four er so hour ride on up to Durango"

He smiled, "I'm going to do that. I need to sleep in a bed. I'm not use to sleeping on the ground."

"Yeah, I can tell that by your eyes. You've lost a lot of sleep. Aztec now has two hotels and five saloons."

"One hotel and one saloon will do just fine."

The next afternoon he rode into Durango on a very tired horse. He slowly rode up the street looking at hitch rails in front of every saloon. "What the hell am I doing? If they're still here their horses would be in a livery."

He stopped a man that was waiting to walk across the street and asked where the livery is. "One is two blocks over to the east. The other one is on River Street five blocks west. Just a half block from that Clear Water Saloon and Bordallo. Big gambling hall an' hotel went in there. Lots of nice-looking women."

"Thanks." He knew if those men knew about that and was still in Durango, that's where they would be.

He rode that way looking for the livery first. He knew his horse was in bad shape and needed food and lots of rest.

He rode right past that big gambling hall and smiled. "Has to be a lot of rich folks in Durango."

He stopped at the livery door and the hostler walked out. "Dad gum Mister, looks as if that horse was about to quit on you."

"Yeah, he's about come as far as he can today."

"Mine, I'd ah stopped thirty miles back."

"He's not yours! Water, feed and stall. I'll let you know how long I'll be leaving him."

He unsaddled the horse and walked him in a stall, but never even thought of looking for those four horses he got for the Lee's and Morgans to ride.

As Gomez walked off, the hostler watched shaking his head. "Man like that ought'a not even own a horse. Needs his liver kicked out, treating a horse this'a way." He patted the horse and gave him an extra scoop of grain.

Gomez walked into a very busy saloon with men in suits standing around talking and patting each other on the back.

About midway of a row of tables, he saw the Lees and morgans sitting with a bottle on the table and a deck of cards being shuffled.

They were busy watching cards and didn't see Gomez until he stopped at the table. Louis looked up with his mouth wide open. "What the hell? What er you doin' here?"

"Thought it time I got the hell out of Bernalillo." He pulled a chair from the next table, as Charlie moved over.

As he sat down, Louis asked, "Yeah, bet there was a big stink when they found we'd robbed that bank again. Lindal, go get the man a glass so I can pour him a glass of mighty good whiskey."

As Lindal got up, Gomez said, "Yeah, but me saying that cowboy shot Ted and me putting bounty hunters on his tail, that brought more trouble than I knew I could handle."

"How's that?"

"It turns out he has a U.S. Marshal as his uncle. He showed up and right off proved that kid didn't shoot Ted."

"Hell, we know that, it was that teller."

Gomez looked at them. "You wanting to get even with that kid for bringing you in, just got a U.S. Marshal on all of our tails."

"Well I'll be a son of ah gun! And you brought him right here to us! Of all the damn stupid…"

"Naw, naw now you know I'd never do that. He has no idea which way y'all rode out of Bernalillo. He said it would be a couple days before he could go looking for y'all. He had to go for help."

"Gomez! If you follered us, by damn so can he! We ride come mornin' an' don't stop runnin' until I know for damn shor he ain't on our tails."

Reese said, "Yeah, if he went for that little cowboy what got us, I damn shor know good'n well we're in trouble. Ain't no stoppin' that little sucker."

Lindal was back with that glass and heard that. "A damn bullet can stop him! Yeah we ride just so far then pull them into an ambush an' kill ever one of um. In any of these mountains that'll be easily done."

Louis said, "Yeah, it might come to that, but not unless we just have to. Folks in Bernalillo will know he came after us. That marshal wind up dead they'll know we done it. Ain't no way of out runnin' U.S. Marshals for very long. Them suckers don't stop."

Gomez said, "Yes, and your grandmother made sure they have pictures of everyone of you. I say head to country were there is no telegraph. There's lots of towns north of here like that. That train out there is the problem. That line will have telegraph lines all the way to California and Oregon."

Louis barked, "We ain't goin' to California er Oregon either one! Lotta places in Colorado, Wyoming er Montana that don't have telegraphs. Now shut up about it so I can think."

Louis was now very worried, as he had never heard of anyone getting away from U.S. Marshals. Yeah, and Gomez could have just given that one the right trail to follow. "Of all the rotten…"

Lindal said, "We could be in for one hell of ah rough ride, don't you think?"

"Hell yes, we are now. Who would have thought that damn kid had a marshal for his uncle?"

"Maybe that's where that kid got his nose an' know how. He shor didn't quit 'til he got us."

"One thing, they ever do catch up, they'll have one hell of ah gunfight. They ain't takin' me back without me killin' a few of um first."

"I still think we ought'a sucker them into a bushwhack trap an' get it over with. You know we're gonna have to kill um sooner er later."

"Yeah, speck yer right. We'll ride come mornin' an' find us the goodest place. Might take ah while."

Gomez said, "Now Louis, we don't even know if he'll ever show up here in Durango."

"Stay an' find out if you want. The four of us will ride an' keep ah eye on our back trail."

"No, I'm riding with you. If he did show up, I'd have no chance on my own."

They sat around that afternoon then walked into the dining room for supper. Louis had been thinking hard. Not for one minute had the thought of that marshal left his mind.

He looked over at Gomez. "Now you think he's two days back, if he did come this'a way."

"Yeah, he said two days before he could get his help. I rode out at noon that next morning after y'all left. That's why I was less than a day behind y'all."

"I think I've come up with an idea that might give us more time."

Forks were stopped half way to mouths, as they all listened. "Tonight, we'll hit small saloons lookin' for men that might want'a make ah few dollars. Maybe three er four men for a hundred apiece could see we have no trouble from a U.S. Marshal."

Gomez smiled, "Yes, I like that idea. As a law man I know men on the run are looking for an easy dollar. I can describe the marshal, and y'all can describe the kid that brought y'all in. I think that might work."

Reese said, "We still don't know how much help he went after. What if it's ah whole posse?"

"Yeah, well what else can we try except ride and keep ridin'. We'll try this then if it don't work, we'll ride like hell an' set up our own trap. I just know he's gotta be stopped, somehow."

Lindal said, "Then let's finishin' eatin' an' get to lookin' for the right men. The quicker we find um the better I'll like it."

As they walked from that dining room, Shorty, Casey, Travis and Ben rode up to the livery in Aztec. As they unsaddled horses, Shorty asked the hostler about those men, saying two would have arms in slings. Then a night later a Spanish fellow might have rode in asking about them.

The hostler smiled, "Right all the way around. An' that Spanish feller rode out for Durango right after sunup this morning. Seemed worried about somethin'. Kept looking back out that door even as he saddled his horse. Like he's afraid somebody would ride up. Guess that'd be you four."

"Naw, he's after those four men just as we are. He catches um first I'd say he'll get dead, quick. He's ah sheriff an' they broke out'a his jail an' tied him up. Then they went an' robbed the same bank again they's in jail for robbin'. I'd say he's pretty well ticked off. Ought'a stayed in Bernalillo."

As they walked up to the café to eat supper, Ben said, "I don't see how we done it but we just picked up a day and a half in just over ah hundred twenty miles er so."

"Well Ben, you noticed we didn't run our horses, just stayed to a steady lope. That way we didn't have to stop ever ten miles er so an' rest um up for ah half hour er so. By lookin' at their tracks back there, they run ah couple miles then slowed them horses to ah walk for ah mile. They lost ah lot'a time doin' that. We rode up to them stage stops before middle afternoon. That's where they'd stayed the night."

"Yeah, I see that. We only had to rest our horses when we stopped an' watered um."

As they ate supper, Louis and those men walked to the rough part of Durango and the second saloon they went into, saw three men, unshaven with low tied guns on their hips.

"Lindal, y'all take that table right over there. I'll get a bottle an' be along."

He walked to the bar and when the bartender saw him, he walked over. "Bottle of yore best whiskey an' five glasses."

All three of those men turned their heads and looked at him. They saw that tied down pistol and nodded their heads as Louis said, "Howdy fellers."

He opened that bottle and reached over pouring their glasses about the third of the way.

They all three smiled, "Say, thanks feller."

Louis walked on to the table setting the glasses down. Pouring drinks around, he pulled out his chair and sat down.

"They'll be over after a bit. I'd bet that's the best whiskey they've ever tasted."

After those men emptied those glasses, one walked over to Louis's table with the empty glass in his hand.

"Uh, y'all ranchers? I mean cowboys can't afford that kind'a whiskey."

Louis said, "Naw, we rob banks."

"Huh? Yer kiddin'."

"Yeah, kiddin'. Care for another?"

"I'd thank you for it."

Louis reached over and poured his glass about half full. "What kind'a work do you boys do?"

"Well now, that's hard to say. Not much of anything I don't guess. Work's hard on ah man's what I've been told. Never tried it myself, 'cept with this forty-four. Pretty good with it."

"I'll say, now that's mighty interesting. I was just looking for a few men that knew how to use pistols or rifles." He smiled.

"You was! I mean you are?"

"Yeah, I'd say easy work and I'd pay a fifty-dollars for each man."

"Fifty dollars! You pullin' my leg?"

"Nope, shor not. I mean if yer interested. Bring yore friends over an' I'll lay it all out. Lindal, you an' Charlie an' Reese move to that table over yonder an' let the fellers sit down. We're gonna talk business."

Louis and Gomez questioned them, making sure they would do what they were being paid to do. The one called Luke smiled, "If we wadn't flat broke, we'd take out ah marshal anytime for nothin'. I hate law that can go past town limits to catch ah feller just 'cause he robbed ah bank er somebody."

The descriptions of Shorty and Casey were laid out where a blind man would almost know them when he saw them. "Now I'd say they won't make it before late tomorrow er the next day. Now we don't know exactly how many there'll be, but at least them two an' maybe a couple more."

"Don't matter how many, they'll not get past us. We know ah good ambush spot no more's ah four er so miles south ah town. Used it ah bunch ah times."

Louis reached in his pocket and counted out one hundred and fifty dollars. "Best y'all get out there an' go to lookin' as soon as you have breakfast in the mornin'. We ain't gonna ride out 'til afternoon, but if they show up 'fore then, you come in an' let us know how many of um you got. If there's more than them two, make shor they'll be yore first shots."

"You can count on us we'll stay out there 'til after dark if we have to."

"Now might not be tomorrow, er might. I don't know how far back they'd be."

"We'll wait, we won't be in no hurry."

After a bit they all went to bed, Shorty and the boys were already sawing logs. They would be on the road as soon after breakfast as they could saddle their horses.

As they ate breakfast Shorty said, "We ride out at five-thirty er so, we'll ride into Durango a bit after nine, before ten anyhow. Them fellers stayed in ah saloon 'til midnight er later they might just be gettin' up. Catch um when they come out of ah café, maybe."

"That or they've rode on for Mancos er maybe Cortez." Travis said that and looked at Shorty.

"Could I reckon, hope not."

They did ride out just as it turned orange in the east. "It'll be cool ridin' all the way. This is ah good stage road so we'll make good time."

Shorty and Ben were a couple horse's lengths in front of Casey and Travis when Shorty hollered back. "Maybe another half hour an' we'll grab us ah cup of coffee then hunt men. Wonder if Gomez found um."

Less than a mile after him saying that, Travis hollered, "Ambush!" As he dived, taking Casey out of his saddle. Shorty had grabbed his rifle diving to his left. He looked up and Ben was sitting there looking all around. Shorty grabbed his arm and jerked him down just as a rifle slug whined over his head.

They all four got off the road and under cover as six or more shots hit nothing but trees. Travis called up, "Can you see um Shorty? Up yonder to the left sun hit off ah rifle barrel."

"Naw, see smokes all. Looks like three of um though. You said that dark ledge?"

"Yeah."

"Yer right, that's where they are, y'all keep um busy while I circle around an' blow the hell out of ever damn one of um."

Ben asked, "Want me to go with you?"

"Naw better not. See if you can make it to yore horse an' get yore rifle without gettin' shot. That's in pistol range so make um keep their heads down."

Casey looked over at Travis, "Thanks brother, saved my butt again."

"I don't think they's shootin' at yore butt." They both laughed and opened fire with their pistols.

Ben yelled, "I think y'all got one of um! Shor looked like he went down."

"Shorty'll know if we did in ah few minutes. Keep shootin' for ah couple more minutes then stop so we don't hit Shorty."

CHAPTER TEN

It took Shorty a while to work his way around behind them. When Travis and them quit shooting, he heard one of those men ask, "Luke, think we got um? They quit shootin'."

"Just why in the hell don't you walk down there an' see! I can't figger why they jumped off their horses before gettin' up here closer where we could'a got um easy."

Shorty knew this wasn't Louis or any of those other men they were after. Now to find out why the ambush. With his forty-five in his hand walked right up behind them and stuck that pistol barrel right in the back of one of their heads.

"It's cocked, what do you say all of you just drop those rifles and I won't have to blow a couple of yore heads off. Up to you, matters not to me."

Rifles were dropped and they stood raising their hands. Casey smiled, "He got um. Let's go give him ah hand."

They walked over getting their horses and Dunnie and saw Shorty was walking them down to the road.

Luke was mad as he glared at Shorty. "Yer pretty damn sneaky. Oh, yer that marshal."

"Yep, pick up those bridle reins and take us ah walk down to the road. Y'all thinkin' ah bout robbin' a few cowboys?"

"Huh?"

"Was y'all gonna try an' rob us?"

"Hell no, we was gonna kill ya."

"Any special reason?"

"Well yeah, we's paid to get it done. Y'all rode up quicker than we's thinkin' er we'd got set better than what we was."

They got down to the road just at Travis, Casey and Ben came walking up leading horses. Kit said, "Be damn Luke, they ain't nothin' but kids. Wonder why Louis an' nem couldn't ah took care of um."

Shorty said to Ben and Casey, "Y'all hold guns on um while they drop them gun belts. Then y'all pick um up and we'll all head into town an get um locked up. I mean unless y'all want to dig three graves."

"Now hold on, Marshal! Dang, don't go an' do somethin' like that. We're got an' causin' no trouble."

"Alright, if yer shor you want it that'a way."

"Oh yeah we do! Don't we Carl?"

"Uh huh, onlyest thing we didn't get to spend one bit of our fifty dollars."

Casey smiled, "Boy howdy y'all work cheap. We're worth at least two hundred apiece. Shorty maybe even five hundred. Don't you think so Ben?"

"Darn right, every bit of that, if not more."

As they headed into town, Shorty asked if Louis still had his three helpers with him. "Yeah, four in fact. Just him an' the Mexkin sit there with us an' told us who to shoot."

"There ain't none of um Mexkin!"

"Shor's hell is! Fifty maybe with ah big gut. Yeah, Gomez is what he was called."

"What! You mean... Well I'll be damn, Gomez!"

Casey asked, "Then you think he was in on it from the start?"

"Looks like. Luke, was they all friendly like? Did Gomez have his pistol?"

"Yeah, they's just sittin' there drinkin whiskey… You know, that was the best whiskey I ever drunk in my whole life. Bet it'll be ah while 'fore I get more."

"I'd say so. Tryin' to ambush ah U.S. Marshal is frowned today. Amount of time you get in jail will be up to ah judge."

"Well at least we'll be fed, I hope."

Shorty laughed, "Yeah, but none of that good whiskey you had last night."

As they rode into town, Charlie started walking from the café first. He stopped dead still and Louis bumped into him almost knocking him out that door. "What the hell did you stop for?"

"Look comin' up the street then ask me that again."

Louis looked and quickly stepped back inside. "Out that damn back door, now!"

Charlie and Louis bumped into Gomez, and Lindal as they rushed for that back door. Gomez half yelled asking, "What the hell did y'all see?"

Charlie over his shoulder said, "That marshal bringin' in Luke an' nem."

"Oh damn!"

Out that back door they went, half running for the livery. As they slapped saddles on horses Lindal said, "I by damn think it's time we stopped him. We wait across the street from that sheriff's office an' blast um as they come out that door."

Louis said, "Yeah, yer about that dumb alright. How'n the hell far do you think we'd get? That sheriff has shotguns and rifles and could hold off an' wipe out half the damn cavalry. We ride now and keep ridin'. We'll make Mancos today, at least."

Charlie and Reese had to have help with their saddles, but all were now mounted and headed out the back of the livery. The hostler had stood right there that whole time and heard every word they spoke. "Bet ah pile of horse droppin's them are

outlaws, must be runnin' from the law."

He headed for the sheriff's office in a fast walk. The hardware store owner hollered, "Hello, Lum."

"Huh? Oh yeah, howdy." He rushed on by.

"Now that must be important. I've ever seen Lum move that fast." He shook his head and continued sweeping the walkway.

He went thru that door, "Sheriff I just... Oh sorry, didn't know you'd be busy."

"That's alright Lum, we were just finishing up. Did you need something?"

"Well yeah, sorta."

"And that is?"

"Five fellers hurried in and slapped saddles on horses an' said they'd be in Mancos by night."

"Yes, I suppose they could be."

Shorty asked, "These fellers, one of um ah Mexkin an' ah couple of um usin' slings."

"Wye yes! How'd you know?"

"Cause them's the bank robbers we're after."

"I knowed them was outlaws by the way they was actin. Yep, just knowed it for shor."

Casey said, "Come on! I'd bet we could catch um!"

"Hold on Casey, didn't y'all just get ah horse shot out from under ah deputy?"

"Well yeah but…"

"This feller said they's headed for Mancos. When they see nobody on their tails they'll slow down. They see somebody they'd try to shoot um an' most likely get horses instead. Dunnie is worth more to me than all that bank money. Naw, we'll go slow an' easy an' let um mess up one more time an' that's when we'll get um."

"Yeah, know yer right. We gonna ride today?"

"We are, grab a quick bite to eat an' head out. Just stay far enough back they'll not know we're there."

Louis and other four men were already two miles up the road and had slowed their horses. Reese looked at each of them then said, "Boys, I don't think this marshal will ever quit 'cause we put his nephew in danger. Made him awful mad I'm feared."

"Yeah, that kid ought'a been shot right off."

Gomez grinned saying, "I tried it and got my pistol shot out of my hand. That little sucker could have drilled me dead center. He ain't no killer, that's for sure."

"If they keep comin' you may get yore chance again. I damn shor ain't goin' to no prison just for robbin' ah bank."

Gomez jerked his head around and looked right at Louis. "We might should have thought of that before we robbed the bank. It is against the law, you know. You either get shot or go to prison if caught."

"Yeah, but with you bein' law an' all, we knowed we'd not get caught. Who in the hell would'a ever thought grandma would'a come up with them pictures?"

Gomez said, "We get caught and live thru it you'll get your picture taken again. They do that now at all prisons. That's so if you somehow break out, that picture is sent everywhere. Most escaped prisoners are now caught within the first week, and most of them killed in a shootout."

"How'n the hell do you know all of that?"

"All that information is sent to all marshals and sheriff's offices."

"No more! Say no more on it! He shor's hell ain't gonna catch us. He does I'll blow his damn head clean off. Wait an' see if I don't."

Louis tried not to let it show, but he sure as hell was worried. If some kid can get them once, a marshal could do it easier. Yeah, and he just might come head on with his pistol blazing hot lead.

"Kick um out, we've gotta get miles between us."

Shorty led out three quarters of an hour later. "Travis, you did a darn good job spottin' that ambush. I'd say don't close yore eyes. These fellers are about to panic and'll be even more dangerous."

Ben asked, "Think if they're cornered, they fight?"

"Oh hell yeah, fact is they won't even have to be cornered. They see any of us they know gotta slap leather. That's why we have to see them first."

Louis and those men rode hard and rode into Mancos right at dark. Taking care of very tired horses,

Charlie looked at his. "Darn it Louis, we're gonna have to stop pushin' these horses that hard. We don't they'll quit. Mine just about has the blind staggers right now."

"Yeah, but they'll rest up overnight. We'll head out right after breakfast in the mornin' an' set us up a damn good trap on that creek eight er so miles this side of Cortez. We now know there's four of um. We lay out that trap just right, we can knock all of um out'a their saddles with our first four shots."

Lindal looked over saying, "Wonder why them three fellers wadn't able to get um."

Gomes said, "Still drunk and didn't hit them with their first shots, I'd think."

Louis said, "I'd say yer right. We shor's hell won't be drunk er have ah hangover either. One drink tonight is all we're havin."

Reese wasn't smiling as he said, "Two drinks wouldn't hurt an' you know it."

"I said one drink! We've never had anybody like them boys on out tails before. Sober we have ah chance, half-drunk we don't."

Gomez said, "I'm with you on that. I've gone against a lot of drunks that beat me to the draw but couldn't even hit the building behind me."

Lindal laughed, "Yeah yer slow alright, I've seen you draw."

"Maybe so, but I sure as hell hit what I'm shooting at! That's a hell of a lot more than I can say for most outlaws. They get jumpy and just shoot at anything."

They ate supper then walked over to the saloon and had one drink, just as Louis had said they would do.

It was just coming on dark as Shorty and them set up camp on the east bank of a small creek, several miles southeast of Mancos.

Casey asked, "Couldn't we have just rode on an' made Mancos before stopping?"

"We could have, and maybe got shot as we rode into town in the dark. Even Travis's eyeballs can't see that good in the dark."

The next morning when Louis and those four men were leaving Mancos, Lindal asked, "What do you think of me waitin' around a few hours an' see if they do show up? If they do an' ride on into yore trap, I'd be behind them with my rifle."

"I'd say you do that there's no chance of a one of um comin' out alive. Just don't you let um see you. You'd have no chance at all. Stay far enough back, if they see you, they won't know yer follerin' um."

"Worry about y'all, not me. Y'all don't get um with yore first shots it'll be up to me to stop um."

As he pulled back and rode between buildings looking for a good spot where he could wait and watch the road, Gomez said, "That brother of yours sure is a thinker. I'd never thought of doing that."

"Yeah, he's good with that rifle too. Them four's as good as dead right now, they do show up. Wait'll you see the trap I have planned. A jack rabbit couldn't live thru it."

Reese said, "Yeah but if we miss with our first shots, jack rabbits don't shoot back."

"Will you just shut the hell up! I know what I'm doin, I don't miss! Yore right arm ain't shot, so you can shor's hell still use yore rifle. Yeah, an' Charlie too. An' that's exactly what you'll do by damn."

They got to that creek and on the far bank was a low rock bluff. "We get our horses out'a sight over behind that bluff an' we'll have plenty of cover. Won't have to shoot more'n ah couple hundred yards as they stop to water their horses."

Shorty and them stopped at the café and ate a good breakfast and was told yes, five men had breakfast and rode out no more than an hour and a half ago.

As they mounted and headed out, Shorty said, "We can kick the horses out just ah dab an' close the gap a might. I'd say even as early as it is they'll make Cortez, and'll hit a saloon for a few drinks."

They hadn't gone a mile when Casey called up to Shorty, "Picked us up ah tail as we was leavin' Mancos. Wanted to wait an' make shor he's follerin' us, he is. We slow down or speed up he does the same. We get out'a sight right up here aways, I'll wait on him."

Shorty said, "Yeah, you do that. I'd say the other four of um has one hell of ah trap set up down here not too far."

He thought a second. "Heck yeah! An I know where it'll be. There's ah creek up here 'fore we get to Cortez that has ah bluff on the far side. I'd be ah wooden nickel that's the spot."

Casey said, "Then maybe this un that's follerin' us can give us ah hand. Y'all wait up yonder around that next bend. Won't be long."

Casey hid his horse and waited no more than ten minutes when Lindal came slowly loping along. With rifle cocked and ready, Casey stepped out in front of that horse.

Lindal put his heels to that horse's sides and jumped him straight at Casey. Casey quickly switched and had that rifle by the barrel and as Lindal tried to pass, he swung it with everything he had. He hit Lindal just below the throat sending him backwards over that horse's rump. He landed on his hands and knees, but before he could grab his pistol, Casey landed with both feet smack dab in the center of his back.

He went face down in the dust of that road as Casey grabbed his pistol. Casey then backed off, rifle again at ready. "Bet that hurt just ah dab, huh?"

"Go to hell."

"Let's play nice now, I could have just shot you right off. You know Lindal, it's hard to believe just how dumb you fellers really are. Now get the hell up an' walk toward yore horse. You grab for that rifle it'll be the last dumb thing you try."

He walked over picking up his reins. "Now around to yore right where I have my horse tied."

Casey eased back and jerked Lindal's rifle from that scabbard and said, "Mount and you might think that horse is fast. Nope, can't out run ah bullet an' I'd just shoot you in the back."

They both mounted and rode slowly on down the road. Casey said, "When I told Uncle Shorty we had a tail, he told us where Louis an' nem has a trap set up. Oh, I'd bet ol' Gomez is the brains behind y'all robbin' that bank. Guess he's as dumb as y'all are."

"You'll think dumb when Louis puts a slug in you."

"Oh I think not. We'll have a little surprise of our own. An' yer gonna be the number one helper."

They rode around that bend and there was Shorty, Travis and Ben waiting. Shorty said, "Never a doubt.

Now let's get on to that next creek an' undo their trap. Casey, you thinkin' what I am?"

"Most likely. Lindal will be in his saddle an' I'll be sittin' behind him with my pistol or his rifle in his back."

"Right you are. They'll see that and it'll take a few minutes for um to figger out what to do. When they jump up, we'll try makin' shots count."

Lindal said, "Damn you, yer gonna get me shot."

"Naw, yore brother ain't gonna shoot you. Maybe they'll just give up an' throw down their guns."

"Don't bet on it. He'll run an' come back for me."

It was almost two hours before they came in sight of that bluff. They couldn't see the creek yet, but knew exactly where it was. "Alright Casey, get up there behind him. Travis, see to his horse."

Casey dismounted and walked over to Lindal's horse. "Get that boot out'a that stirrup."

Casey mounted then said, "Travis, pitch me one of them rifles. Y'all stay back out of range until they jump up to save Lindal."

Ben said, "What if they see he's been got an' just high tails it?"

"Then we'll only be chasin' four instead of five. Lindal here will keep a cell company in Cortez while we go after them."

Casey said, "Alright Lindal, let's ride in all slow like. Remember, any stupid thing you try to pull will just get you dead."

They rode to the creek and stopped. Louis was screaming his head off. "He was got! Damn it Lindal was got!"

Gomes said, "I don't see none of the others. One of us should be good enough with a rifle to pick that cowboy off."

"Don't be stupid, Gomez! Them other three are just out there waiting for us to try somethin' stupid. Let's ride, they'll put Lindal in jail in Cortez and go on after us. We'll sneak around an' bust Lindal out then ride in another direction."

Gomez said, "Damn it we're in a good spot! They can't get to us up here. Let's just stay and take them on. If we get one or two, maybe three we could..."

He quickly put his rifle to his shoulder sighting down that barrel. Before Louis could get over to him and stop him. he pulled that trigger. That slug took Lindal smack dab in the middle of the chest. Before he could fall from the saddle, Casey grabbed him, keeping his body in front of him.

Louis screamed, "Naw! Naw! You stupid idiot you went an' killed Lindal!"

"It's his own damn fault for getting caught! Now I can..." Louis shot him in the side of the head.

As he was knocked sideways, Louis bent down and ripped his shirt open, grabbing that money belt. He headed for his horse with Charlie and Reese right behind him not saying one word. They were too damn sacred to talk.

They jumped in those saddles and headed down that creek with horses in run.

Casey was making that horse walk backwards until he could get under cover. Shorty hollered, "Could you see what's goin' on up there? After that rifle shot a pistol was heard. Did that shot come close?"

"Naw, but I could hear yelling. That rifle shot got Lindal, he's dead."

Casey let go of Lindal and he fell from the saddle. Casey slid of the horse's rump and looked down. "Yeah, never knowed what hit him."

Shorty walked over saying, "Bet a dollar that wadn't Louis what shot him. Y'all wait, I'll be back."

CHAPTER ELEVEN

While Shorty was working himself across the creek and up behind that bluff, Casey and Ben loaded Lindal belly down across his saddle. Ben said, "Yer just lucky he was in front instead of you."

"Yeah, shor didn't think nobody would shoot him though. They must be gettin' desperate to shoot one of their own, hopin' they could get me next."

Shorty worked his way around, but was pretty sure they had pulled out as there were no more shots. He saw one horse, pulled his pistol and slowed. He got to the horse and patted it, looking all around.

"Now why'd they leave this... Oh..."

He walked over and saw Gomez had been shot in the head. "Well Gomez, guess you learned too late not to shoot a feller's brother with him standin' right beside you. Gotta have help loadin' that two hundred pounds er so."

He walked over to the top of the bluff and called out. "Casey! I need you an' Ben up here!"

They heard him and waved, heading that way.

When they got up there, Casey said, "Well I know what that pistol shot was. Must'a been Gomez that shot Lindal. Yeah, an' Louis didn't take too kindly to it. Look, his shirt is undone. Think he had on ah money belt?"

"I'd say so, now Louis has all the money. Need y'all's help gettin' him up in that saddle."

Louis, Charlie and Reese had slowed their horses. Charlie asked, "Why in the hell would Gomez shot Lindal?"

Louis said, "Yeah, I ought'a shot him when he showed up. Had'a Lindal would still be alive. I knowed he brought that marshal right to us. Still can't figger how Lindal was got by that kid."

Charlie asked, "Uh Louis, what do you think ah about us just givin' ourselves up?"

"What? Are you out'a yore damn mind?"

"Naw, what the hells ah few years in prison? Better that than bein' dead. You know that marshal ain't gonna quit 'til we're all got."

"We'll be in Cortez in just a bit. I'll let y'all split Gomez's money and y'all do what you want. I'll keep that last robbery money. I'm headed for Utah and get lost for ah whole year. All I've gotta do is stay ahead of that marshal until I get in that Utah canyon country. He'll never find me."

"Yeah, what are you gonna eat, sandstone?"

"Lot'a wild life in there, I'll eat."

Reese said, "I'll ride with you, but shor's hell ain't gonna get in no gunfight when he does catch up."

"Then what the hell good would you be? What about you Charlie? To save yore life would you use ah gun?"

"Naw, I'm done. Just wore plumb out. I'll sit in that saloon 'til he walks in and arrest me. Won't say ah word where you went. You goin' er stayin, Reese?"

"Guess I'll stay with you, brother. Louis, you keep all the money, we won't be needin' none in prison. I'm with Charlie on stayin' alive."

"I damn shor ain't dead yet! Alone I'll know how to run an' hide like nobody you've ever seen. I'll drop by ah grocery an' get plenty ah grub then ride hard an' fast."

An hour later Louis tied a huge sack of groceries behind his saddle. Turning he said, "Well boys, wish y'all luck. Just sorry as hell Lindal ain't here to ride with me."

Charlie said, "Louis, if he comes down to it don't get dead. Remember prison for ah few years might not be so bad an' you'd be free ah gain."

"It'll never come down to that. He comes after me in that canyon country, I'll get him with my rifle."

As he rode off, Charlie and Reese stood there watching after him. Reese said, "Well Charlie, looks like the end of the line is near for us. Knowed it'd happen one day. Glad we never killed nobody. At least we won't hang."

"Yeah, let's tie the horses right in front of the saloon. We'll walk in there an' order the best whiskey he's got. It'll be our last for a good while."

They did that, and as Charlie paid for that bottle and got two glasses, he unbuckled his gun belt, looking at Reese. Best you do the same."

They handed those belts and pistols to the bartender. "Won't be needin' these no more."

"You mean yer givin' um to me!"

"Yeah."

"Then here's your money back on that bottle."

As they took a table and poured drinks, Shorty and the boys stopped at the livery and asked where the undertaker was.

The hostler said, "Yeah, see you need him. One block over then west right behind the sheriff's office. How'd it come about you shootin' um."

"We didn't. Their friends did."

"Some friends! Glad none ah mine's that'a way, least I hope the hell not."

They dropped the bodies off at the undertaker with Shorty saying he was sure they had plenty of money on them for the burying.

Circling around they went in the sheriff's office. "Howdy Marshal, after somebody?"

"I am, they might'a stopped down yonder in the saloon. If they did there'll be gun play. I'll try like hell not to get nobody else shot."

"Guess I'd better walk along. I know where the doc is if you do have to shoot um."

"We'll take our horses along incase they do make it to a back door. Bullets flyin' I shor's hell won't chase um."

"Smart man, let's go."

They walked down and before walking in the saloon, Shorty made sure that forty-five was setting loose in the holster. The sheriff said, "Guess you know um?"

"Yep an' they shor's hell know us."

They walked in and spread out. Four tables over Charlie called out, "Howdy Marshal, got time for ah drink er are you in ah hurry?"

Shorty was ready for anything as he looked around for Louis. They all walked over, with Reese saying "Pull out some chairs. We won't be finished with this bottle for a good little while. Shor would like it if y'all would help us with it, 'fore you jail us."

Casey walked around behind, looking. "No guns, Shorty."

Shorty, Casey and the sheriff pulled out chairs. Travis and Ben did the same at the next table. Shorty asked, "Care to tell me what this is all about?"

"Don't mind tellin' at all. Lindal is dead, so's Gomez. No need in us bein' dead too. Never killed nobody so don't guess we'll hang. We just couldn't see gettin' in ah gun fight an' maybe dyin' over ah bank robbery. So, looks like we're caught. Gave our pistols to the bartender when we walked in. Rifles are on our saddles right out front. Didn't figger you bein' ah marshal you'd shoot down ah unarmed man. Now how about that drink?"

"Hell, may's well. Bartender, five more glasses."

The bartender brought those glasses, but Ben, Casey and Travis said, "Thanks, but we'll have beer. Not old enough to drink that whiskey yet."

The bartender smiled, "Smart boys. Be right back."

They all relaxed and started talking. Shorty asked, "Did Gomez shoot Lindal, then Louis shot Gomez?"

"Yep, that's how it went down alright."

"Care to tell me where Louis got off to?"

"Naw, you know we can't do that. All I'll say is west. We tried talkin' him into givin' up so he don't get his self dead, but he wouldn't hear of it. Tried to tell him livin' even in prison for ah few years beats the hell out'a bein' dead forever."

"You both seem to be cowboys, how'n the hell did you get tied up with the Lees?"

"Oh we was all cowboys 'til Gomez got voted in as sheriff. He let us know in ah hurry they's easy money to be had. No way we could ever get caught 'cause he was sheriff. Then that damn kid right there chased us all over hell's half acre an' got me an' Reese here without killin' us. When Gomez faked that jail break, we thought we had us another chance of stayin' out'a jail. If Lindal an' Louis hadn't told Gomez that kid shot his deputy, we'd been out'a jail in ah week. That big lie is why you was called in, to keep that kid from hangin' for somethin' he didn't do."

"The deputy didn't die."

"No matter, Gomez would'a hung him anyhow for shootin' that gun out'a his hand."

"Did Louis pick his self up any more men here in town, er did he ride out alone?"

"By his self. Said he knowed how to run an' not get caught. Now Marshal, he said he'd not be took. He has all that money from both bank robberies."

"Then sooner er later with all that money, that means saloons, drinkin', gamblin' an' women. Take a while, but yeah, I'll get him, just hope it's alive. A man like that can't stay holed up by his self for long."

They talked and after a bit Reese picked up that empty bottle. "Well Marshal, that's about it. How about us walkin' over to that café an' I buy us all a steak dinner. I'd say it'll be the last steak we get to eat for ah long time. Sheriff, yer even invited."

As they ate, Shorty said, "Travis, come mornin' I'll be ridin' northwest alone. I want y'all to head back to Bernalillo with Reese an' Charlie. Just be damn careful, it's a mighty long way."

Charlie said, "Marshal, as we said we're thru. We'll cause no trouble. At least we're alive, that's the main thing. We're still young enough when we get out, we'll make ah nother start. May even find a job on ah ranch where they'd hire two brothers."

Charlie said, "Funny thing Marshal, me an' Reese never robbed one of them banks. Lindal an' Louis did. We just sat on our horses an' waited outside."

After their meal, they all walked over to the sheriff's office. Reese said, "Marshal, our horses are tied right in front of the saloon."

"Yeah, we saw um. We'll get um took care of same time we feed an' water ours."

The next morning, they went to the sheriff's office and got Charlie and Reese. Then all walked to the café and ate breakfast and talked. Shorty said, "Now I think Charlie and Reese here will be no trouble. Just don't take a chance they might change their minds. I'd say they don't have to be tied when in the saddle, but shor's hell at night, in ah hotel er beside yore campfire."

Reese said, "Yeah they'll have to do what they think's best, but our word no trouble of any kind."

Casey smiled, "Stop worryin', yer actin' like mama now. Just you watch out for yore self. I'd say Louis is the most dangerous of the whole bunch."

"Spect yer right on that. If all goes well, I'll see y'all in ah week er so, maybe."

They walked out going to the livery and saddled horses. Shorty mounted and headed northwest toward Dove Creek. The boys mounted and headed back toward Durango.

Travis said, "May's well kick um out boys. We'll be drinkin' beer in Durango by the time the sun goes down."

****

Louis had camped a few miles before reaching Dove Creek and was now in a café eating breakfast. His eyes never left that door. The waiter asked, "Waiting on someone?"

"Hell no, why'd you ask that?"

"You keep looking at that door like you was expecting someone."

"Well, I'm not. Gimme another cup ah coffee."

He rode west twenty minutes later. In his mind he knew that marshal was comin, but how far back? Would he have time to make Monticello? Could he make it south to that Indian town of Blanding then southwest into the canyons before he caught up?

"What if I went north? Gobs of canyon lands around and west of Moab, I'll do it. I'm not chicken like Reese an' Charlie. Givin' their selves up like idiots just to go to prison. By damn not me. He comes at me he has ah fight on his hands."

Shorty made Dove Creek just before noon and stopped and ate. Then he rode west keeping a steady pace. He knew he could make Monticello by sundown, but which way would Louis go out of there. "I'd guess north most likely toward Moab and Green River.

Nothing south but Blanding and desert canyons plumb way down into Arizona."

Louis rode into Monticello and ate while his horse rested. After watering the horse at the town pump, he headed out that stage road north.

Five hours later he rode up to a stage stop called La Sal Junction. As he took good care of his horse, Shorty was just riding into Monticello.

Travis, Casey, Ben and the Morgan brothers had already taken care of their horses and were eating supper. Charlie said, "Guess when we're done here you'll maybe buy us ah beer, huh?"

"Yep, had that in mind." Travis said as he took his last bite. He paid and they walked down and across the street to the saloon.

That beer was good and cold so they decided two would be even better. The sheriff walked in seeing them. "Well I'll be dog, y'all got um!"

Four men standing at the bar, turned watching and listening. The sheriff asked, "Where are them other three? Yeah an' the marshal? They all dead?"

"Naw, just two of um. Shorty went on after the only one that got away. We're takin' these two back to Bernalillo where that bank was robbed."

The sheriff said, "Yeah, that wire said they got off with over twenty thousand."

Reese laughed, "That was the first robbery. The bank got half of that back. That kid there saw to that."

"What happened to the second half?"

"That was Sheriff Gomez's half, he kept that. That second time we robbed the same bank, we got another forty er so."

"The hell you say! Don't guess you had time to spend much of it. Did you say a sheriff got half of the first robbery money?"

"Yeah, the whole thing was his idea."

"Got to spend hardly any at all. Casey here just couldn't be shook, just kept on our tails 'til he got us all but one. Say sheriff, you got ah empty cell they could leave us in tonight? That'd shor beat bein' tied er handcuffed to a bedstead."

"I sure do and it's mighty nice. It'll give the boys a break."

As they talked, those four men turned back to the bar, looking at one another. One nodded, "Time we took ah leak."

They walked out back to the outhouses with one saying, "I think it's about time we got rich with about forty thousand dollars. We'll be saddled up in the mornin' and while they eat breakfast, we'll beat it out to that big bend about three miles down the road. Them big boulders ah hundred er so feet to the left will make us ah good spot. They'll hear us good when we yell out."

Another said, "Damn, was we lucky er what? Just happened to be right there when that sheriff let ever body know two of them boys is bank robbers. Yeah, an' never got to spend none of that money."

Another laughed, "Yeah, an' them other three boys brought it right to us. Mighty nice of um I'd say."

The last one said, "Yeah, three kids won't be no trouble at all. I'd say we won't even have to kill um."

"Naw, scare the hell out of um's all."

After the second beer, the sheriff walked with them up to his office and put Charlie and Reese in a cell. Travis said, "We'll come get you for breakfast."

"Don't forget!" Charlie laughed, as did Travis.

****

Louis was at that stage stop and had supper and now sat with a glass of whiskey in his hand. He looked at it, then raised it to eye level. "I'll miss the hell out'a you Lindal. It'll get mighty lonely without you to talk to. My fault, should'a shot Gomez right off."

The next morning, he rode from La Sal Junction about the same time Shorty left Monticello. Travis, Casey and Ben had gone up to the sheriff's office and got Charlie and Reese and after breakfast saddled horses and rode out.

Charlie and Reese were in front and Travis had told them to hit a good pace he wanted to make Durango before night fall.

Not quite three miles later, Charlie slowed and looked down at his horse's leg, then stopped. The others rode up as he dismounted and lifted that horse's left foreleg. Casey was closest and asked what was wrong.

"Don't turn to look, but we have four rifles pointed right at us."

"Where?"

"A couple hundred yards up on the left. I just happen to see when one of um stood up. I'd say y'all get yore rifles pulled out'a them scabbards an' dive off below that bank. Me an' Reese will be right behind you."

Travis said, "I heard that an' he's right. Up yonder behind those boulders. Ben, Casey, at the count of three jerk them rifle and dive to the right out'a them saddles. One, two, dive!"

They all did and Luke was watching, "Now why'n the hell did they do that" "Stark can you see um?"

"Naw the went over that bank torge the river. Think they went to fill canteens?"

"Now how'n the hell would I know that…" Casey just bounced a bullet off one of those boulders. "Hell no! They saw us! Open fire!"

"At what dummy? We can't even see um to shoot. They have as good ah cover as we do."

"Now if that just don't beat the blind hell out of everything. Just ah bit closer is all we needed."

Luke said, "Damn it I want that money! I'm gonna give um ah chance to throw that money out then we'll let um ride off an' not shoot."

"Luke, you have got to be as damn dumb as one of these boulders. They know we can't get to um. They can stay right there 'til hell freezes over. Ain't one damn thing we can do 'cept get shot."

"I'm gonna try anyhow. They's just kids, maybe I can scare um into it."

He cupped his hands to his mouth and yelled, "All we want's the money! Throw that out an' you can ride! We'll not shoot y'all!"

Ben asked, "What the hell's he talkin' about?"

Casey laughed, "Gotta be dumb thinkin' cowboys have more'n a few dollars."

Casey hollered back, "You mean all twenty dollars of it!"

"Hell no! That forty thousand them two robbed from that bank!"

"Yer crazy as hell! We don't got no forty thousand! The marshal is still after the feller that got away with all that money."

"I don't believe you! Yer lyin!"

"Go to hell! Come an' get it!"

Travis said, "Alright, I'm runnin' to my horse an' stay to the off side. I'll pick up the reins an' take um over this bank where they can't be seen. We'll walk um down to the river out'a sight an' just ride off."

Reese said, "Better let me an' Charlie go for the horses. We'll do it an' not get shot. Y'all with them rifles keep their heads down."

"Hell yeah, go for it. Casey, Ben open up."

One would shoot then the other as Reese and Charlie ran and got all five horses. Over that bank they came and not one shot had been fired at them.

They stood down behind that bank with smiles. Travis said, "Good job, let's go."

They led the horses until they not only couldn't be seen, but were out of rifle range. They mounted and headed out, horses in a run.

Stark looked at Luke, "Wonder why they quit shootin'. Think maybe they're out 'a bullets?"

"Hell, I don't know. One thing, they shor don't scare." He hollered, "One more chance, then we're comin' for that money! You'll all die!"

No answer so he slowly peeked around that boulder. "What the hell?"

Stark asked, "What? They throw out the money?"

"Hell no, their horses is gone an' I'd bet they are too."

"Naw, naw! Now by damn that just ain't right! What'll we do?"

"Get on back to town an' forget it. An' damn, we was so close to bein' rich. I mean just that close."

As Casey, Travis, Ben and the Morgans rode, Casey was talking, "Thanks, Charlie. We wadn't even thinkin of an ambush. Another hundred yards an' they'd had us for shor."

Charlie laughed, "Yeah, an' we all might'a been in trouble when we couldn't come up with any part of that forty thousand."

CHAPTER TWELVE

Louis made it to Moab right at noon, stopped and ate. As he walked from the café, he looked up the street and saw a saloon and farther down two blocks was a huge sign saying livery.

This time of day he knew not too many fellows would be in that saloon, but the hostler always knew what was going on.

He got his horse and rode to the livery and dismounted. Just inside those opened doors sat an old man in a rocking chair, looking to be half asleep.

He called out, "You asleep?"

The old man looked up, "Not now I ain't. What dah ya want?"

"Lookin' for a feller er two what really knows them canyon lands."

"No gold er silver down there er it'd already been found. So why are you askin' about it?"

"What business of that is yours?"

"None, just thought I'd ask. Earl Culp an' Smithy Combs, both ah them would know them canyons better'n anybody else around, I reckon."

"Know where I'd find um?"

"Earl is up yonder at the saloon. Smithy is in jail 'til sundown."

"Why sundown?"

"Cause that's when the sheriff'll let him out."

"What's he in there for?"

"Workin' over ah card sharp."

"What happened to the card sharp."

"Got put on the mornin' stage out'a town."

"But why then was Smithy put in jail?"

"When the sheriff tried pullin' him off that sharp, he turned an' knocked the hell out'a the sheriff before he saw who it was."

"Thanks, guess I'll go up and talk to Earl."

"You do that." He leaned back in that rocker and pulled his hat low over his eyes.

Louis rode up to the saloon, walked in and stopped at the bar. Two men sat at a table talking, one man farther down the bar turned his head and looked at him. Another man sat at a table alone with an empty glass about middle of the table.

They bartender walked over, "What'll you have?"

"First, which one of them fellers is Earl Culp?"

"That' un!" He pointed to the one at the table.

"I'll take a bottle, good stuff, not crap."

"It'll cost a dollar."

"Get it!"

He took that bottle and his glass and walked over to Earl's table. "Care if I sit an' we have us ah drink?"

"Sit, an' pour."

The glasses were a third full when Earl said, "Yer wantin' somethin', what is it?"

"Heard you know them canyons."

"I do."

"What'd it cost me you takin' me down in there for a couple days?"

"Twenty dollars an' you furnish the grub. When er you want'n to go?"

"After two drinks I want to ride."

"In ah hurry, huh?"

"Kind'a."

"Alright drink up an' we'll go to the livery an' get my horse. You already got grub?"

"Yeah, plenty for ah week er ten days."

"Whiskey?"

"Two bottles an' we'll take this un along."

Less than an hour later they were at the livery. The hostler said, "Howdy Earl. Gonna take him?"

"May's well, nothin' else goin' on right now. I'll see you in ah few days I reckon."

They rode out, horses in a slow lope. Earl asked what he was looking for. "I'd like to find me ah spot with water close an' where I can stay out'a this hot sun. Oh an' I'll need grass for my horse. Might stay around there a good while."

"Know just the spot, no more'n six er so miles. Got some old Indian ruins over lookin' ah darn good creek. Lot'a grass all along them banks. Easy to stake out yore horse. Only take us ah less than couple hours as it's ah easy ride right down that creek."

He turned his head and looked at Louis. "Care to say how many's after you?"

"What makes you think anybody's after me?"

"Ain't dumb. Noticed how you liked that whiskey. Wadn't bein' chased you'd be in ah saloon ever day drinkin' an' playin' poker. None ah my business, I work for you."

"Maybe four, was anyhow for one hell of ah long time. My brother's dead, the other two boys quit, give up. Not me I ain't goin' to no prison."

"Guess you'll want'a get the one that killed yore brother sooner er later."

"Already got him."

"Good, that's good an' one less to worry about. Any good with that hog leg an' rifle?"

"I am, good enough to stay alive."

"Don't nobody ever come down this'a way no more that no gold was found. Just me an' Smithy ever now an' ah gain just to get the hell away from town. Them Indian ruins is big, really nice summer er winter. Stay cool er warm.

"Me ol' Smithy has laid up there lookin' out when it was rainin' cats an' dogs. Horses was in one of them building's stayin' dry."

"I might want to be here up to ah couple weeks. One of um what's after me is ah U.S. Marshal. They have all the time in the world. If he's still on my tail, a week from now he'll be in Salt Lake City."

"Yeah, had ah marshal on my tail years back."

"What happened to him?"

"Nobody knows, heard he went off in these canyons an' got his self lost. That's what I heard anyhow. Nobody ever saw him again."

"Did you help him get lost?"

"I did an' done ah good job of it."

Just under two hours later they were at those ruins. Louis had never seen anything like this. "Man, this is ah good spot. Ever hear why the Indians left?"

"Naw, figger them cavalry boys killed the hell out'a all them braves an' the women ah kids starved to death er just went on down that creek into northern Arizona. That's what I figger anyhow. They stayed to the creek they'd made it alright."

They unloaded the supplies and placed them in a building with a roof, then unsaddled the horses and took the saddles inside. Then they walked the horses down to water.

Louis said, "Looks to be ah lot'a deer around here, all these tracks."

"Yeah, hunters only come down here in the fall an' thin ah few of um out. Other'n that they're left alone. One thing ah feller would never go hungry."

****

Shorty rode into Moab just before dark and took care of Dunnie. The hostler looked at him as he removed the saddle. "On somebody's tail er just ridin' thru?"

"Tailin. Figger he's rode on by now, but if he's here I'll catch him in one of them saloons. Care if I look at all them horses?"

"Go ah head, he know you?"

"He does."

"Then just to stay out'a unwanted gunfights, why don't you take off that badge? I'd say there's at least ten er twelve boys in them saloons that's on the run. No need you gettin' shot by none ah them."

Shorty laughed, "Good Idea. What kind'a law do y'all have?"

"Tough but fair. Always gives the feller the benefit of the doubt. Lie to him an' he finds out you've got one hell of ah problem."

"Best I eat me some supper first off then go for ah beer. That sheriff visits which one ah them saloons?"

"All of um sooner er later. The Bad Lands Water Hole right over yonder is his favorite."

"Hell of ah name for ah saloon."

"You won't think so if you drink some of his home-made whiskey. Bad enough to make ah healthy dog puke up his guts."

"He don't also make his own beer, does he?"

"Naw, bet he's thought of it though. Oh, Sheriff Rhodes will be over there any time now to buy Smithy Combs a drink."

"Why'll he do that?"

"Smithy gets out jail in another quarter hour. Been locked up for two days. Sheriff'll buy him ah drink. Matter ah fact a quarter hour from now I'll be over there drinkin' my own beer."

Shorty smiled, "I'll still be eatin' supper, just don't drink it all."

A good half hour later Shorty walked into a noisy saloon. Everyone had already welcomed Smithy and asked how the sheriff treated him.

"Mighty good, good grub. When I get hungry again, I think I'll up an' slug somebody else."

He laughed, the sheriff didn't. Shorty got his beer and sat at a table listening to all the talk. The hostler was there and got to do talking of his own.

After a bit Smithy was looking all around. "Anybody seen Earl lately? Don't see him."

The hostler said, "Saw him right after dinner as he rode off takin' ah feller down in the canyons."

"Why would he want'a do that?"

"Reckon he's getting paid to do it."

"Say how long he'd be gone?"

"Naw, a few days is all."

Shorty had heard all of that and asked, "Was that ah big feller ridin' ah big bay gilding?"

"Shor's heck was! Low gun on that right hip. I told him there wadn't any gold down there, they went anyhow. Course he didn't look like no miner no how. Looked like ah run ragged cowboy. Shor has lost ah lot ah sleep as of late."

Shorty asked, "Anyone else around here that knows them canyons?"

Before all the other men in there could say Smithy, Sheriff Rhodes did. "Smithy here does. Maybe you'd want'a go down there an' take Smithy with you. It'll get him out'a my hair for ah few days at least."

"Ah come on Sheriff. You know full well I had to whip upon that card sharp after he went an' cheated the way he did. Sittin' there grinnin' like he'd just eat the last piece of cake."

Shorty said, "Smithy when you get time, I'll buy you ah drink if you'd sit ah talk ah while. I just might want'a go down in them canyons."

Smithy looked at him. "It'll cost ya cowboy."

"Figgered it would. I'll pay what it's worth."

"Never turned down no money, be right there."

The sheriff had finished his drink and was ready to go home. "Cowboy, try to keep him out'a trouble."

Smithy walked over and pulled out a chair. "What's on yore mind?"

"I'm after that feller Earl took into the canyons. I think he's lookin' for ah place to hole up awhile 'till I get tired an' call off my hunt, er ride on lookin' elsewhere."

"Sounds like it could down to ah shootin'."

"As soon as he sees me it shor will."

"Then you'd be dead. Too many places down there he could see you comin' for ah mile an' you shor's hell couldn't see him 'til you was shot."

"Now that don't sound so very good. But dog gone it I've gotta get him. He's ah bad un."

Smithy looked at him. "Now the right kind'a money I'd ride down there an find um an' see if you could get to um er not without bein' shot."

"What for more money would keep you from tellin' him I'm after him?"

"Ask anybody in here, they'll tell you Smithy Combs never goes back on his word. I ain't got much but never lied to nobody yet an' don't plan on startin. Shor I like money an need some right ah bout now, but you come with it first."

"Name yore price."

"Ten dollars, one day."

"You find um, I'll make it fifty."

"What? Yer puttin' me on! Cowboy, you don't look like you'd have fifty dollars."

"What do you say we meet for breakfast in the mornin'? I'll pay you the ten right up front. You find um and get back we'll figger out how I can get him without takin' lead."

"By dog you've got ah deal. Still fifty if you get him?"

"Shor is, I'm another feller that don't go back on his word." They shook hands and Shorty bought two beers.

The hostler walked over. He had heard every word said. "Cowboy, he'll do you ah job. Knowed him for years. His word is good. Care to let folks know what yer after that feller for?"

"He looked at me all wrong, even nodded his head with a sneer as if he didn't like me."

"Huh? An yer goin' after him for that? You have to be about as crazy as a slapped around horsefly!"

Smithy looked at him. "Dirk, yer an idiot! That was just his way ah tellin' you it's none ah yore damn business why he's after him."

"Oh well then, that's better." The whole bar busted out laughing, including Dirk.

The next morning after breakfast, Shorty handed Smithy ten dollars as they walked to the livery for his horse. As he saddled up, he said, "Wouldn't think they'd get too awful far from town. I should be back fore night anyhow."

"Think Earl will let Louis shoot you?"

"Naw, no cause. Earl knows I ride off down that'a way ever now an' ah gain. So does he."

He rode out and already had those Indian ruins in mind. "Best spot down there far's I'm concerned. Bet they went no farther. Might have to stay a bit an' jaw but that cowboy will buy me dinner. Yep, 'cause I'll be back in town by then, if that is where they are."

He rode down in the canyon following two set of hoof prints. An hour and a half later he smiled as he saw two horses staked out on tall grass. As he rode up Earl called out. "See Rhodes let you out. What er you doin' down this'a way."

"Went for ah ride just to get out'a town. No call in Rhodes lockin' me up just for kickin' the hell out'a that card sharp. If I's a gunnie I'd shot the sucker."

Earl laughed, "Yeah an' ol' Rhodes would had to hang you shor nuff."

"Then I guess it's best I didn't shoot him. What er you doin' down here anyhow?"

As he said that, Louis walked from the house holstering this pistol. Smithy said, "Whoa now! Was I about to get shot?"

"Naw, Louis is ah bit jumpy is all. When I told him who you was he membered Dirk mentioned you same time as he did me. Gonna step down ah while?"

"Naw, I'm ridin' on down ah good ways. Don't circle too far off I might stop back by this evenin'. Y'all got anything to drink?"

"Yeah, ah couple bottles."

"Then I guess I'll not be seein' you in town for quite ah while."

"Naw, we'll be in Friday night. Big poker games Louis wants to get into. Feller what's on his tail ought'a rode on way 'fore then."

Louis asked, "You happen to notice four cowboys ridin' in, one of um might'a been wearin' ah badge."

"Naw, got out'a jail late last night an' rode out after breakfast. Saw nobody I didn't know."

"Best I get, might circle around up top an' see if I can run into that big elk herd. I do I'll just ride on back that'a way an' see y'all in town Friday night."

"Yeah, so long, Smithy. Glad to see Rhodes didn't keep you."

Just before noon, which was just short of five hours after Smithy rode out of the livery, he was back unsaddling his horse. Dirk asked, "Find um?"

"I'm back, ain't I?"

"Well yeah."

"Then I found um. Bet Shorty is already over yonder in the café."

"He is, saw him walk in a short while ah go."

Smithy walked in the café and right to Shorty's table. Shorty looked up, "Back already I see."

"You see good, how about buyin' a poor man his dinner?"

"Yer not poor, I give you ten dollars this morning."

"But if I's about to tell you what you want'a hear, you would buy, right?"

"Right. Waiter another bowl of this stew."

When Smithy told him he found them right off, Shorty asked if he could get to them. "Nope, it's in ah narrow canyon an' they could spot you comin' for a quarter mile. But there's hope yet."

"Now what's that supposed to mean?"

"They'll be in town Friday night for them big poker games what goes on ever Friday."

"Friday! This is only Tuesday!"

Smithy looked at him, "You want um without gettin' shot er not?"

"Well yeah."

"Then it'll be Friday. Friday afternoon we'll ride out yonder where they'll come out'a that canyon. You take Louis an' I'll keep Earl off you. I mean after you give me that fifty dollars, I have comin."

"You'd stand against a friend?"

"Marshal, at the time yer my friend. I work for you. Me an Earl will leave you two be. I'll see to that."

"How'd you know I's ah Marshal?"

"Louis said one of the four men after him would be wearin' ah badge. Bein' as there's only one of you, I figger yer the marshal."

"That's me, and thanks for the help."

He counted out and handed Smithy fifty dollars. "Now Shorty, you'll still need me come Friday afternoon.

Without me Earl would shor'a hell help the feller what paid him."

"Spect yer right."

CHAPTER THIRTEEN

For Shorty that week past slow with nothing to do but sit and wait. Several times he started to say to hell with it and head down in that canyon, but he's talk himself out of it. He was sure Smithy had been right and all he would do is get his self shot.

Thursday right afternoon, Travis, Casey, Ben and the Morgans rode to a stop in front of the sheriff's office in Bernalillo. Charlie said, "I shor do hope they made that little guy Ted sheriff. He'll make ah good un."

All this way, they had not been cuffed or tied. They had given their word no trouble, and kept it. As they started dismounting, Ted, with his shoulder still in a sling stepped out of the office.

"I see you got um. Where's Gomez? You know he rode out after them the next day."

Reese said, "Louis put a bullet in his head for shootin' Lindal."

"Reese! That was his job, get everyone of you!"

"His job was to see we wadn't caught an' tell he was behind that first robbery."

"What? I don't believe you."

Travis said, "He told it straight. Gomez was behind it all. When he let these boys out'a jail, Louis an' Lindal robbed the bank again. Shorty is still after Louis, 'cause he has all the bank's money including what Gomez had on him. That was half the first robbery, his cut."

Casey said, "Ted, you go easy on these two. They saved our hide twice. If not for what they did they wouldn't be here now an' maybe ah couple of us dead er at least have ah few bullet holes."

Ted looked at them all, "Then I'll get them locked up and maybe it would be best if all three of you went over and talked with the judge. It'll be up to him to go easy or hard on them."

"We'll do that, but 'fore you lock um up, I'd like to buy um a good meal an' maybe a beer er two. You ain't in no hurry, are you?"

"No, but I'll have to go with you and I don't drink."

They ate and walked over to the saloon and took a table. Men turned their heads mumbling to each other. One got up his nerve and walked over. "Ted, ain't that two of them bank robbers?"

"They sure are."

"Then what the hell are they doin' in here 'stead of over yonder in jail?"

"Having a drink, what does it look like? After having steak and taters, they just had to have a couple drinks."

"Of all the... Now I'm gonna..."

"You'll do nothing. Just back off and leave things along. They'll be in jail soon enough."

"Well... I'll leave it up to you Ted."

"Thank you, Walter, things are not always as they look. I have my reasons for doing this."

"Suppose you do. When'll that worthless Gomez be comin' back."

"He won't, he went and got himself killed."

"No loss there. Fact is that's good news. Maybe, just maybe they'll make you sheriff."

Ted laughed. "I doubt that, they'll want a much older man."

An hour later Charlie and Reese were behind bars and both thanked Ted for letting them eat a good meal and have a couple drinks.

Travis, Casey and Ben were talking with the judge and told him everything. "Now I'm tellin' it true Judge, them boys helped us er we shor nuff wouldn't have made it. Shor do wish you'd go as easy on um as you can. They'd never got tied up with that first bank robbery if it hadn't been for that crooked Gomez."

"I'll dwell on this and talk with the marshal when he gets back. Perhaps he will catch Louis Lee and bring most of that money back."

Casey said, "You can bet on that Judge. He won't stop 'til he gets him."

"Are you boys going to hang around until the trial?"

"We are, I'm shor Uncle Shorty would want us to be. We'll let Gus know we're here so he can send his deputy out an' let mom an' dad know we're alive."

****

The next day, Friday, Shorty and Smithy ate dinner and rode southwest of town around one or so. "Well

Shorty... You don't mind me callin' you Shorty 'stead ah marshal.do you?"

"Nope, all of my friends call me Shorty."

Smithy smiled, "Well then, right over yonder is where we'll wait. Horses can be put well out of the way an' we'll be in the shade 'til they get here. I'd say pretty quick now. They'll want'a eat somethin' 'sides beans for they start drinkin' an' playin' poker."

They sat in the shade and talked when around three o'clock Shorty said, "Two horses comin'."

"Yep, heard um. Best get set."

Louis and Earl were just walking their horses and twenty or so feet in front of them, Shorty stepped out in the trail, forty-five in his right hand.

Horses were jerked to a stop and both men's hands went to the butt of their pistols. Smithy hollered, "Best you stay out of it, Earl. That's ah U.S. Marshal."

Both hands stopped without grabbing those pistols. Louis said, "Yer not takin' me alive, Marshal."

"Oh, now I think I will. It'll be up to you as to what kind'a shape yer in. Now raise yore hands."

"Hell no! I'm gonna step out'a this saddle an' if yer not ah yeller livered polecat you holster that pistol an' give me ah chance."

"Now why in the hell would I want to do that when I have you covered. Raise um er I go to shootin'. First yore gun arm, then the other an' both legs if I have to. Yer goin' back to Bernalillo, alive."

Louis went for his pistol and shorty shot him in that wrist. Louis screamed, as Shorty said, "Raise um! You still have one arm an' two legs I hadn't shot yet!"

"You've got me! You just wait, one day I'll get out'a prison an' I'll damn shor look you up first thing."

"Then I'd say that's the day you die. Smithy, think you can bring our horses?"

"Already headed that'a way."

When they got to town and Louis was walked in the sheriff's office, Shorty said, "Do I search you er do you just hand it over?"

Louis dug in his shirt and got that bank bag and took Gomez's money belt from around his waist. "Sheriff, we'll be ridin' at sunup. Can you see he's fed early?"

"He will be. Guess you have a couple weeks in the saddle gettin' him back?"

"Naw, three days to Cortez then another to Durango. There I'll put him on the train and be in Bernalillo three days after that. Right now, I'm gettin' over to that saloon and buy Smithy a drink. That sucker is worth havin' ah round."

"Yeah, if he'll quit punchin' the hell out of fellers."

"I heard that feller needed it."

"He did, but by damn I didn't! He knocked the crap out'a me too."

Just over a week later, Louis was in the cell next to Charlie and Reese. His wrist was bandaged and he was still mad as hell. He talked thru the bars. "If y'all hadn't turned chicken an' come on with me, he'd never got us."

"Oh, he'd got us alright, but we could'a been dead. You wouldn't be goin' to prison with a ruined right wrist if you'd give up when we did."

"He's ah coward! He wouldn't even draw against me. I'd got him for shor."

"Uh huh, I believe that. We go to trial day after tomorrow. Guess we'll be sent to Canon City for ah few years. But beat's the hell out of the cemetery."

Shorty took that money over to the bank and picked up that reward for Travis, Casey and Ben to split. Those boys all did a good job

Two days later trial was at ten in the morning. The judge and jury listened to Ben, Travis, Casey and U.S. Marshal Shorty thompson. Also Ted got to say it was the teller that shot him, while shooting at Lindal and Louis. It was Gomez that said Casey Pascoe was the one that shot him."

The jury was sent to their room to reach a verdict. Ten minutes later they were back and the jury foreman gave the verdict of guilty with the suggestion of leniency for both Morgan brothers.

The judge smiled, "You gentlemen were thinking along the same lines as I was. You four men, stand and face me. Louis Lee, I here-by sentence you to ten years at hard labor in the penitentiary at Canon City.

Charlie and Reese were in a sweat, they were hoping for less than five years each.

The judge cleared his throat and looked at Charlie and Reese, then at the Pascoe boys and U.S Marshal

Shorty Thompson. Every one of them were holding their breaths.

"Charlie and Reese Morgan, I here-by sentence you to five more day in the town jail. Court dismissed!"

Shouts went up from everyone, including the banker. Shorty and Travis had told him if not for those two, the money may have never been recovered. They gave themselves up instead of getting into a gunfight they were sure they couldn't win. They wanted to kill no one.

Charlie turned and looked right at Casey and Travis. "Thanks fellers, this won't be forgot."

The next morning Shorty and the Pascoe's, with Ben riding along rode into Albuquerque and let Gus know the outcome.

Gus said, "There was never a doubt in my mind of the outcome, with the best two bounty hunters and a number one U.S. Marshal on their tails."

Ben asked, "What about me?"

"Spend your part of that reward money and be glad you all got back in one piece. Pascoe boys, I'll now let you two buy the beers being as I'm the one that sic'ed you on them to start with."

Shorty said, "Yeah Gus, an' what got me involved was wrong bullet wrong man. When Gomez sic'ed bounty hunters on my nephew, that was all of um's downfall. With lots of extra help we got um."

Novels From Paul L. Thompson

(#108) U.S. Marshal Shorty Thompson – Wells Fargo Is Easy To Rob

(#107) U.S. Marshal Shorty Thompson - The Dead Trail

(#106) Grandpa and The Kid

(#105) U.S. Marshal Shorty Thompson - I'll See You Both Dead

(#104) U.S. Marshal Shorty Thompson - Almost The Fastest Gun

(#103) U.S. Marshal Shorty Thompson - Montrose Colorado

(#102) U.S. Marshal Shorty Thompson – Rough Trip Back To Boise

(#101) U.S. Marshal Shorty Thompson - White Oaks - A Town With No Law

(#100) U.S. Marshal Shorty Thompson – Five Thousand Dollars

(#99) U.S. Marshal Shorty Thompson – Caught One Crooked Banker

(#98) U.S. Marshal Shorty Thompson – A Bad Decision

(#97) U.S. Marshal Shorty Thompson – The Last Man

(#96) U.S. Marshal Shorty Thompson - Gold and Silver – A Robber's Paradise

(#95) U.S. Marshal Shorty Thompson – Marshal Shorty Please Help Us

(#94) U.S. Marshal Shorty Thompson - Keith Aurzada - Lawyer Gunfighter

(#93) U.S. Marshal Shorty Thompson - Cimarron River - Rustlers Hideout

(#92) U.S. Marshal Shorty Thompson - The Fifth Man

(#91) U.S. Marshal Shorty Thompson - A Bit Of Crooked Law

(#90) U.S. Marshal Shorty Thompson - You Get Five Years

(#89) U.S. Marshal Shorty Thompson - A Kidnapped Education

(#88) U.S. Marshal Shorty Thompson - She's Alive, Not For Long

(#87) U.S. Marshal Shorty Thompson - Six Years Wait For A Showdown

(#86) Two Sister's Revenge

(#85) U.S. Marshal Shorty Thompson - Clayton New Mexico

(#84) U.S. Marshal Shorty Thompson - If Hell Ain't Hot Enough

(#83) U.S. Marshal Shorty Thompson - Mister You Was Shot In The Head

(#82) U.S. Marshal Shorty Thompson - Ms. Deborah Has Been Kidnapped

(#81) U.S. Marshal Shorty Thompson - One Sweet Kiss Can Kill You

(#80) U.S. Marshal Shorty Thompson - We're Gonna Die Ain't We Danny

(#79) You Shot Me Once! Never Again!

(#78) U.S. Marshal Shorty Thompson - Bartie Longshore - I Sentence You To Twenty Years

(#77) U.S. Marshal Shorty Thompson - Animas City - A Town to Forget

(#76) U.S. Marshal Shorty Thompson - Mister I'll See You Dead

(#75) U.S. Marshal Shorty Thompson - Don't Ever Make Old Men Mad

(#74) U.S. Marshal Shorty Thompson - Deputy U.S. Marshal Betty McCabe

(#73) U.S. Marshal Shorty Thompson Meets U.S. Marshal Hopper Scranton

(#72) U.S. Marshal Shorty Thompson - Kill Every Witness

(#71) U.S. Marshal Shorty Thompson - Monty Long - The Long Hunt

(#70) U.S. Marshal Shorty Thompson - Evil With A Gun

(#69) U.S. Marshal Shorty Thompson - The Widow Martha Camden

(#68) U.S. Marshal Shorty Thompson - I Know Who Back Shot Mister Fred

(#67) U.S. Marshal Shorty Thompson - Dead Is All You'll Get

(#66) U.S. Marshal Shorty Thompson - Blood Over The Horizon

(#65) U.S. Marshal Shorty Thompson - Deputy Sheriff John Dunow

(#64) U.S. Marshal Shorty Thompson - A Winter Too Cold For Gold

(#63) U.S. Marshal Shorty Thompson - No Justice for the Innocent

(#62) U.S. Marshal Shorty Thompson - Pure Raw Justice

(#61) U.S. Marshal Shorty Thompson - Tillie Jane From Hillsboro

(#60) U.S. Marshal Shorty Thompson - Marshal Shorty Turns In His Badge

(#59) U.S. Marshal Shorty Thompson - Yer in the Wrong Town Mister

(#58) The Wherry Gang Saves Christmas

(#57) U.S. Marshal Shorty Thompson - Death Is All That's Left

(#56) U.S. Marshal Shorty Thompson - In the Middle of The Colfax County War

(#55) U.S. Marshal Shorty Thompson - Billie & Bonnie Coleman - Women To Deal With

(#54) U.S. Marshal Shorty Thompson - One Crooked Town

(#53) U.S. Marshal Shorty Thompson - Cora Laredo - One Mad Woman

(#52) U.S. Marshal Shorty Thompson - I'll Hunt You Down

(#51) U.S. Marshal Shorty Thompson - Take Aim - Shoot Straight

(#50) U.S. Marshal Shorty Thompson - When Winter Winds Blow

(#49) U.S. Marshal Shorty Thompson - Keep The Gold - We Keep Our Ranch

(#48) U.S. Marshal Shorty Thompson - Long Trail To Nowhere (continued)

(#47) U.S. Marshal Shorty Thompson - From Texas to Montana

(#46) U.S. Marshal Shorty Thompson - It Takes More Than Bullets

(#45) U.S. Marshal Shorty Thompson - Blood, Sweat and Gold

(#44) U.S. Marshal Shorty Thompson - Black Pearls, Blue Diamonds & Bullets

(#43) A Very Long Time Before Cowboys

(#42) Long Trail To Nowhere

(#41) U.S. Marshal Shorty Thompson - You Think I Shot Him

(#40) U.S. Marshal Shorty Thompson - Revenge of the Bullet

(#39) U.S. Marshal Shorty Thompson - Killers and Outlaws

(#38) U.S. Marshal Shorty Thompson - Little Toby Smith

(#37) Love Is One Shadow Away

(#36) U.S. Marshal Shorty Thompson - Hang Shorty in Leadville, Colorado

(#35) Young Outlaws (almost)

(#34) U.S. Marshal Shorty Thompson - Doug Brown & Shelly Hampton

(#33) William Colby U.S. Marshal Retired

(#32) U.S. Marshal Shorty Thompson - The Road To Chama

(#31) U.S. Marshal Shorty Thompson - Milo Tillie

(#30) U.S. Marshal Shorty Thompson - James P. Retzer - Dentist - New Mexico, Territory

(#29) U.S. Marshal Shorty Thompson - Janice McCord Rides Again

(#28) U.S. Marshal Shorty Thompson - David Graham - The New Gun

(#27) U.S. Marshal Shorty Thompson - Please Don't Leave Me

(#26) U.S. Marshal Shorty Thompson - Cowboy Cody Strickland

(#25) U.S. Marshal Shorty Thompson - The Martin Boys

(#24) Before I Die

(#23) U.S. Marshal Shorty Thompson - Killing Of Outlaws

(#22) U.S. Marshal Shorty Thompson - Whiskers McPherson & Gabriel O'Grady

(#21) U.S. Marshal Shorty Thompson - Janice McCord

(#20) U.S. Marshal Shorty Thompson - This Mountain Is Mine

(#19) U.S. Marshal Shorty Thompson - The Young Trackers

(#18) U.S. Marshal Shorty Thompson - The Wrong Man Again

(#17) U.S. Marshal Shorty Thompson - The Long Chase For Justice

(#16) The Last Gun in Town

(#15) U.S. Marshal Shorty Thompson - Women In The West Did Survive

(#14) U.S. Marshal Shorty Thompson - Young Jessie Owens

(#13) Brothers of The West

(#12) U.S. Marshal Shorty Thompson - When Preaching Is Hell

(#11) U.S. Marshal Shorty Thompson - A Mother's Wrath

(#10) Can Loneliness Last Forever

(#9) One Good Deed

(#8) U.S. Marshal Shorty Thompson - Children Of The West

(#7) U.S. Marshal Shorty Thompson – Malpais

(#6) U.S. Marshal Shorty Thompson - Ride Hard For Rayado

(#5) U.S. Marshal Shorty Thompson - Trouble in Tascosa

(#4) Saddle Mountain

(#3) U.S. Marshal Shorty Thompson - Willow Lane

(#2) U.S. Marshal Shorty Thompson - Silver of the Black Range

(#1) U.S. Marshal Shorty Thompson

PAUL L. THOMPSON

thompsonpaull@outlook.com

www.oldwestnovels.com

Made in the USA
Middletown, DE
21 July 2023

35501850R00159